# The
# Counterfeit
# Coin

# THE CASE

## OF THE

# Counterfeit Coin

### A BRAINS BENTON MYSTERY

### *by* GEORGE WYATT

*Based on the characters created by*
CHARLES SPAIN VERRAL

## *Illustrated by HAMILTON GREENE*

A WHITMAN BOOK
Western Publishing Company, Inc., Racine, Wisconsin

WHITMAN is a registered trademark of
Western Publishing Company, Inc.

# TABLE OF CONTENTS

| | | |
|---|---|---|
| 1 | The Crawling Hand | 9 |
| 2 | The Vanishing Clue | 18 |
| 3 | The Hunt Begins | 28 |
| 4 | Dead End | 35 |
| 5 | Shadowy Trail | 42 |
| 6 | Trackdown | 46 |
| 7 | The Third Degree | 49 |
| 8 | Incriminating Evidence | 53 |
| 9 | Shadowed | 63 |
| 10 | The Face in the Fog | 70 |
| 11 | Dangerous Profession | 77 |
| 12 | Spies at the Window | 85 |
| 13 | Search for a Clue | 93 |
| 14 | Suspicion | 101 |
| 15 | Double Cross | 108 |
| 16 | Secret Operations | 113 |
| 17 | The Crooked Trail | 124 |
| 18 | The Clue | 134 |
| 19 | The Mysterious Warning | 142 |
| 20 | High Tension | 150 |
| 21 | House of Peril | 157 |
| 22 | Escape in the Dark | 164 |
| 23 | Last Chance | 172 |
| 24 | Captured! | 177 |
| 25 | Enter the Police | 183 |

# 1 THE CRAWLING HAND

I don't think I'll ever forget that bottle of soda pop. Not as long as I live.

That's how the whole thing started—with a drink of ice-cold cherry soda. But before it was over—*brother!*—I was up to here in a genuine Grade-A detective mystery, complete with guns, knives, screams in the night and a bumper crop of goose pimples.

First, let me fill you in on a few details. Like my name being Jimmy Carson and that I live in the town of Crestwood in a white clapboard house at 43 Maple Street with my father and mother and seventeen-year-old sister Ann, and that my best friend is a kid genius named Brains Benton.

Except for the thumb of my left hand being double-jointed, I look like a million other American kids my age—brown-haired, brown-eyed, average in height and weight. I'd never stand out in a crowd, that's for sure.

Maybe that doesn't sound like much of a compliment. But it sure helps in my secret profession.

[ 9 ]

You see, I'm a private detective! That's right. I'm a private eye, and so is my friend Brains Benton. In fact, Brains and I are partners. We operate the Benton and Carson International Detective Agency in Crestwood.

And just in case you're the type who thinks that a couple of school kids can't solve crimes and mysteries, I wish you'd seen the *Crestwood Daily Ledger* last July when we cracked the case of the stolen circus. They gave us a big front-page write-up and a splashy headline: JUNIOR SLEUTHS TRAP CROOK.

Of course, it was really Brains who solved that mystery. It usually is. He's the president and mastermind of the Benton and Carson International Detective Agency.

I'm secretary-treasurer. I do the leg work, like keeping suspects under observation and getting fingerprints and rounding up evidence. But when it comes to using the old think-tank, it's Brains all the way.

His real name is Barclay Benton. But the kids at school hung that Brains label on him. They could have called him Red or Skinny or Legs. But a guy has to *earn* a nickname like Brains.

It figured that Brains would be smart. After all, his father is a professor of ancient history at Crestwood College. And his mother's a painter. She's on the staff of the college, too. She teaches art. So I guess Brains came in for a double dose of gray matter.

I've known Brains almost all my life. We're about the same age and we're in the same class at school. And when we discovered that we were both interested in criminology . . . well, that's how the Benton and Carson International Detective Agency came into being.

In my spare time after school I handle a newspaper route for the *Crestwood Daily Ledger*. I mention this fact right here because if it hadn't been for my paper route, I'd never have gone into Doc Saffron's drugstore for a bottle of cherry soda that day. And if I hadn't bought that cherry soda, the Benton and Carson International Detective Agency would never have had a chance to solve one of the most baffling cases in its entire history.

It all began one Saturday morning in April during my Easter vacation. I was out making my weekly collections on my paper route. I always collect from my customers on Saturday morning.

My last call, as usual, was at the Barnes family. They live on the outskirts of Bleeker City, about three miles down the County Turnpike from Crestwood. They moved out of Crestwood a year ago but Mrs. Barnes still liked to keep up with the news and gossip in the *Ledger*.

I save the Barneses for my final call for a couple of reasons. First, I don't want to take the chance of running into that pesky kid of theirs, Binky, any sooner than I have to. And second, Doc Saffron's drugstore is just down the block from the Barneses. After two hours of cross-country pedaling on my bike, a cold bottle of Cherry-Fizz really hits the spot.

Well, everything went pretty much as usual that morning. Some of my customers were out, and some put off paying. But most of them came through. And I was plenty glad that Binky Barnes wasn't at home when I collected from his mother.

I figured it was close to eleven o'clock when I parked my bike outside Saffron's drugstore and went in. There was nobody in the place that I could see, except Doc Saffron himself. I remember thinking that was kind of funny. Doc does a big trade, especially at the fountain.

But the store being empty didn't really bother me. Maybe it would've been better if it had. I might have paid closer attention to that stranger when he came in, instead of waiting until it was too late.

Doc didn't ask me what I wanted. He just waddled over behind the soda fountain, grinned in that crinkly way he has and called out, "One extra-cold bottle of Cherry-Fizz coming up!"

I hoisted myself onto a stool. "Golly, Doc," I said. "How did you *ever* guess I was going to order a Cherry-Fizz, of all things?"

Everybody called him Doc. He was short and bald-headed and sort of ugly, I guess. But you knew he was your friend—just by looking at him.

"Why, Jimmy," Doc said, "it was a clear case of mental telepathy. I read your mind."

"Amazing," I said.

Doc and I always kidded around like that. Of course he knew what drink I wanted. Good gravy, I'd been stopping at his store every Saturday, rain or shine, since I'd had the paper route. And I always ordered a bottle of Cherry-Fizz. I was sort of partial to Cherry-Fizz.

Well, Doc put the bottle of soda in front of me and I dug into my jeans. I was weighted down with change from my collecting. I finally pulled out a dime and gave it to him. At least I thought it was a dime. But as I was taking my first long delicious pull of Cherry-Fizz through the straw, I noticed Doc turn around from the cash register.

"Sorry, Jimmy," he said. "We accept only *American* money here."

He shoved the coin back across the marble fountain top to me. I just sat there looking, and I'm sure my mouth was wide open. Because it wasn't a dime at all.

It was a piece of silver about the size of a well-worn ten-cent piece. On one side was a head wearing a funny kind of helmet. And when I turned the coin over—*creeps!* There was a weird-looking owl with pop eyes staring at me. And alongside the owl were three letters—AOE.

"Hey!" I let out. "Where'd I get *that* thing?"

"Maybe you picked it up somewhere along your route," Doc said.

"Yeah," I said. "I bet that's it."

I got a dime out of my pocket, a *good* one this time, and gave it to Doc. But I kept on staring at that other coin. And the owl stared right back at me.

"I wonder what country it comes from," I said.

Doc shrugged. "Beats me. Maybe it's a rare coin and worth a fortune, Jimmy." He laughed. "But again, maybe you're just out a dime. Better charge it up to profit and loss, and forget it."

*Forget it!* Not on your sweet life. Doc could wisecrack about the coin being worth a fortune—but maybe it was! This called for a quick consultation with my partner Brains. And the quicker the better. Brains knew just about everything about anything. And what he didn't know he could find out.

I took another swallow of Cherry-Fizz to sustain me, then I slid off the stool and headed across the store in the direction of the phone booths. There were two booths against the wall close to the entrance.

I noticed that Doc Saffron had shuffled off to his dispensary at the rear and was out of sight behind the frosted-glass partition. But for some reason, probably because I was thinking so hard about the strange coin, I wasn't aware that anybody else had entered the store until I saw a man standing in one of the phone booths.

That's where I made my first mistake on the case. I should have tried to get a look at that guy's face. Of course, it would've been difficult. I mean, he had his back turned against the closed door of the booth and he was hunched over the phone as if he didn't want anybody to hear what he was saying. He had the collar of his coat turned up, too, and the brim of his black felt hat pulled way down.

Anyway, at that particular moment, the guy just didn't exist as far as I was concerned. I stepped into the vacant booth alongside, dropped a dime in the slot and dialed Brains Benton's number.

I was excited. I had a kind of hunch that the coin might lead to something. I sure was hoping so. The private-detective business had been at an all-time low for some time.

I could hear the phone ringing at the other end. Then, suddenly, a high-pitched irritable voice was shrilling in my ear.

"Hello? Hello? Who is it?"

Of all the foul luck. I'd hoped to get Brains right away. Instead, here was Mrs. Ray, the Bentons' housekeeper. She was a fussy little woman who had a habit of trying to stick her nose into other people's business—particularly Brains'. She disapproved of almost everything about him. She was, as Brains himself once remarked, the kind of person who would make an ideal stranger.

"Hello, Mrs. Ray," I said politely. "This is James Carson. May I speak to Brains . . . ah . . . please?"

"Speak to *whom*?" The peevish voice in my ear went into a sharp zoom on that last word. "There's no one by that outlandish name living at this house."

I kicked myself. I should've known better.

"Excuse me, Mrs. Ray," I said in what I call my marshmallow voice because it's sort of soft and gooey. "May I speak to Barclay?"

"Now then, that's much better," she said. "I believe he's in that dreadful laboratory of his. He's been there since breakfast. Why his parents tolerate it, I'll never know."

There was a buzzing sound which meant that the housekeeper was calling Brains over the intercom he'd rigged up with parts from an old radio.

In a moment I heard my partner's voice say, "Hello?"

"Brains, this is Jimmy," I began.

There was a dull click and I knew that Brains had flipped a switch, putting into operation a special device that stopped Mrs. Ray from listening in on any of our conversation. It was another of Brains' inventions and I think the one that infuriated her the most.

When Brains' voice sounded again, it was clearer and sharper.

"Remember when using the telephone, security is of the utmost importance, Operative Three. Please observe routine procedure."

That was my partner for you. I could almost see him frowning in his best Sherlock Holmes manner.

I'd better explain that when Brains and I are working on a case we're mighty careful to maintain a shield of secrecy. We use cover names when we think security might be endangered. He's known as X and I'm Operative Three. There is no Operative Two.

"Sorry, X," I said. "Operative Three reporting to headquarters."

"State your business, Operative Three."

I waited a moment. I wanted my news to sound impressive. Then, in a tense whisper, I said, "Satellite Zeta is in orbit."

I listened for Brains' reaction. *Satellite Zeta is in orbit* was the secret code that meant important news. But Brains didn't act surprised or amazed or startled. In fact, he sounded, if anything, impatient.

"I assumed you had something of interest to tell me," he said. "Otherwise you wouldn't have called me all the way from Saffron's Drugstore in Bleeker City. Now, what is it?"

Brother, I almost flipped.

"Wait a minute," I said. "How'd you know where I was phoning from?"

"Elementary deduction," he said. "This is Saturday, the day you make your collections. It's now about eleven o'clock. Knowing your routine, you've probably just finished your rounds. When this happens, you invariably repair to Saffron's to enjoy a repulsive concoction known as Cherry-Fizz."

"O.K. . . . O.K.," I said. "You're right. I'm at Doc Saffron's. But how come you knew I had something important to tell you?"

Brains sounded as if he were yawning.

"Simplicity itself," he said. "If your tidings had been merely routine you would have waited until you arrived at headquarters in person. But the fact that you thought it necessary to expend ten cents on a phone call from Bleeker City obviously indicated that your news was important. . . . Now, please, give me the details and make it brief. I'm in the midst of an optical experiment."

But I wasn't letting him give me the rush act! Not while I was holding the center of the stage.

I sat down in the booth and put the mystery coin on the phone-box shelf where I could see it clearly. Then I opened the door of the booth for some fresh air. With the door opened I could hear the man talking in the next booth, but his voice wasn't much more than a mumble. It wouldn't interfere with my conversation.

But opening that door was the second bad mistake I made on the case, although I didn't know it then.

"It's this coin," I said to Brains. "I must have picked it up on my route."

"Be more specific, Operative Three. You pick up lots of coins on your route," Brains said sarcastically.

"Not like this one," I replied.

I gave him a rundown on all the details of the coin—the head, the helmet, the popeyed owl and the three strange letters, AOE.

I was trying my darndest to act casual and nonchalant, the way any experienced detective would, but I wasn't too successful.

"You'd better lower your voice, Operative Three," interrupted Brains. "If you talk any louder I won't need a phone to hear you."

He was always talking to me in that superior way of his. I was about to tell him off when suddenly I noticed that the guy in the next phone booth had stopped talking. I caught a flash glimpse of a face at the open door of my booth. I figured my loud conversation must have disturbed him, so I lowered my voice to almost normal.

"One more thing about the coin," I said to Brains. "There's a funny kind of crack in it. It starts at the edge and sort of points toward the center."

"Hmmm!" said Brains thoughtfully. I could almost hear the gears humming in that redheaded skull of his.

I was waiting for him to come up with something. Then, out of the clear blue sky, I felt it—that creepy feeling you get when you know someone's spying on you.

Call it a guess, intuition, sixth sense. Call it anything you like. But at that moment I was dead sure of one thing.

Someone was eavesdropping.

I turned my head toward the door and there it was—the shadow of a man standing just out of view around the corner of the booth. My hair almost lifted right off my head.

Then something crept in past the folded door of the booth, something on five bony talons like a huge, hairy spider with one black leg.

But it wasn't a spider. It was a human hand—with a *black* thumbnail.

Then, suddenly, the hand made a quick grab for the mysterious coin.

# 2 THE VANISHING CLUE

I yelled!

Brother, I'll bet they heard me clear across the state line.

In the next wild second that hairy hand was yanked back out of sight. And the door of the phone booth was slammed in my face.

That yell snapped me out of it, too. I rammed my shoulder against the door.

But it wouldn't open!

Of course it wouldn't. Those phone-booth doors open *inward*. I lost precious seconds fumbling for the handle. Then the door folded back, and I was barging out into the store.

I saw the figure of the man who'd been in the other phone booth scuttling for the street.

"Stop," I yelled and charged after him.

And then something grabbed my legs and held on!

What it was I didn't know, but I was going down *fast,* and the floor was coming up to meet me.

When we met, *out went the lights!*

To tell the truth, I didn't see stars. But for a moment there, I was on my way into outer space in the vicinity of some mighty colorful planets.

I came to on my hands and knees, shaking my head to clear away the fog. Doc Saffron was standing over me, trying to help.

"My left leg," I gasped. "Something's wrong! I can't move it!"

"That's not surprising," Doc said, dryly. "Your leg's jammed inside a carton."

I looked back and what do you know!

He was right! I was knee-deep in a carton of discarded paper cups.

"Sorry, son," Doc said, apologetically. "I was about to dump that carton out back but I guess I forgot about it."

I yanked my foot out of the box, glad it was still in one piece.

"I didn't see the carton at all," I said. "I was too busy chasing that man."

Saffron looked at me dubiously. "What man? Hasn't been anyone but you inside the store for the past few minutes, son."

"Why, there was a man in the phone booth," I began. "He had a hand like a—"

And then I stopped.

Can't you just see me trying to tell him about that hand crawling along the wall like a hairy spider? Or about those bony talons with the black thumb searching blindly for the mysterious coin?

Would he believe me?

Would *you?*

So I smiled as innocently as I could and said, "I guess I was kinda daydreaming, Doc. I—I thought I saw someone I knew."

Doc Saffron looked at me over the top of his glasses. He picked up the carton of used cups and lugged it toward the back.

"The way you yelled, I thought someone was about to murder you," he said.

Creeps! For one minute there, so did I!

Suddenly I remembered something. The coin! I'd left it on the shelf, unprotected. Did the weird-looking stranger get it?

I dived into the booth—and sighed with relief. The mysterious coin was still there.

From somewhere nearby I heard an excited babbling sound. I looked around and spotted the dangling phone receiver. Brains! He was probably still on the line wondering what happened to me.

I picked up the phone.

"Jimmy! Jimmy, are you there?" Brains was yelling.

"Brains! Wait till you hear what happened." I began.

I babbled out a play-by-play report.

"I'm lucky I wasn't murdered," I concluded.

"A remote possibility," Brains said. "The chances are that the man with the blackened thumbnail owned the coin and only wanted to recover it."

"But if the coin was his, all he had to do was ask for it. I'd have been glad to return it."

"Hm, you've got something there, Operative Three. The fact that the culprit didn't wish to be identified *is* most suspicious and warrants a thorough investigation."

Which is just what I was getting at all the time. But only Brains Benton could have said it in quite that way. Now you see why he's *president* of our detective agency.

"I urgently suggest," Brains went on, "that you report to headquarters immediately. And be on your guard, Operative Three. One attempt has been made to secure that coin. There may be others."

I wet my lips nervously. "Trust me, X," I said. "I'm on my way right now."

As I left the store I passed Doc Saffron and I thought I heard him sort of sigh, as if in relief.

With the coin clutched firmly in one hand, I pedaled like fury and did the three miles back to Crestwood in nothing flat.

Brains lived on Chestnut Drive, four blocks from my house.

But instead of going along Chestnut Drive, I slipped down an alley that led behind the Benton property. In back of the house stood a garage. It was an old building that had been converted from a coach house. The upstairs rooms had once been used as servants' quarters. But Brains' parents had not only allowed him to use them for himself, but also let him turn the whole upstairs into an amazing, up-to-date research laboratory. This lab was the home base of the Benton and Carson International Detective Agency.

When I reached the rear of the garage, I hopped off my bike and shoved it through the tangled bushes on the north side of the old building. Then, after making a careful surveillance of the main house to make sure that Mrs. Ray wasn't snooping, I crouched down and pressed the third nail in the fourth board from the bottom.

Instantly a voice spoke from a hidden amplifier.

"Your name and business." It was a metallic whisper you could barely hear.

"Operative Three reporting to headquarters," I replied. "Official business."

Silently the garage wall opened in front of me as a hidden panel slid to one side. I stepped through and the door closed behind me. At the same time a faint blue light flicked on and I saw the hidden staircase just ahead.

As I climbed the stairs, I heard the faint whir of machinery and I knew the staircase was folding up behind me. At the top another panel opened silently and I stepped into the secret laboratory.

What a place!

Try to imagine the combination of a research lab, a machine shop and the control room of a flying saucer, and you might begin to get the idea.

There were workbenches crowded with scientific equipment —vials, test tubes, microscopes. There were shelves loaded with transformers, dials, tubes and every kind of electronic equipment. Not to mention enough power tools to supply an entire machine shop. Everything was neat, orderly and ready for instant use.

I seemed to be alone as I entered the deserted room, but I knew that I was under observation through the two-way mirror on the far end of the wall.

Then the trick mirror swung aside and there, seated in what he called his "inner sanctum," was X. As usual he was dressed in a long white lab coat. He had been reading and now he came toward me with a thick book in his hand.

"Ah, Operative Three," he said. "You made excellent time. Now, may I have the coin in question?"

I dug it out of my pocket and handed it over. I watched him walk to a nearby bench.

He was tall, and thin as a rail. He had big feet, but he was far from awkward. His hair was an unforgettable strawberry color. His face was thin and he had the kind of nose you'd expect to find on Sherlock Holmes himself. He wore glasses, too; but behind those specs his eyes were blue and razor sharp. There was very little that got past Brains Benton, I can tell you.

Maybe he sounds weird the way I describe him, but if you think this long, skinny drink of water was a weakling and a mama's boy, guess again. He was the best pitcher in the school league, and he held the state record for shutouts and no-hitters.

Not that he was interested in sports, but pitching appealed to his scientific brain.

"Propelling a baseball," he once said to me, after pitching nine innings of scoreless ball, "is a most challenging problem. It involves the application of a variable force to a ballistic missile which must then proceed through an unknown factor of wind resistance toward an indefinite target."

I don't know exactly what that means, but Brains Benton was still the best pitcher in the school league.

He had placed the mysterious coin on a bench and was looking through the thick book again.

"While you were on your way here I consulted the encyclopedia on the subject of numismatics," he said. "Numismatics, in
case you do not know, is the study of coins. It's a vast field,
Operative Three. Frankly, I find myself intrigued."

He leaned back against the bench, put his fingers together
like a church steeple and regarded me solemnly.

"Actually," he went on, "numismatics is a science involving
a knowledge of history, mythology, economics, metallurgy . . ."

"All right!" I didn't want a lecture. "What about this coin?"

"Operative Three," Brains pronounced sternly, "impatience
is not a commendable quality in a criminal investigator."

Having put me in my place, he turned and held up the silver
coin.

"First, let us consider the origin of this coin. The helmeted
head is of Athena, the Greek Goddess of Wisdom. Many Greek
cities used her image on their coins."

"How about that popeyed owl," I asked. "He ought to give
us a good lead."

Brains turned to an open volume of the encyclopedia on a
stand near him.

"According to this article, the owl was the symbol of Athena's
wisdom. It was also the sign engraved on the coins of ancient
Athens."

Brains pointed to the lettering engraved beside the owl.
"Those letters are the Greek symbols for Alpha, Theta and Epsi-
lon—together they are an abbreviation of the name Athens."

He removed his glasses and polished them. "Yes, this is doubt-
less an Athenian coin, minted in the fifth or sixth century B.C."

I grinned. "You're batting .500," I said. "How about that crack
in the metal," I asked. "It sure saw a lot of wear and tear to be
split like that."

Brains smiled. "Ancient coins were often split as they were
being minted. But that notch was probably made by a trader
who had some suspicions about the quality of the coin."

"Speaking of suspicion," I said thoughtfully, "we still don't know why the man with the blackened fingernail wanted that coin so badly."

"Correct," Brains agreed. "There must indeed be something special about it. It might pay to have a closer look at that coin."

Brains placed the coin under an instrument that looked like a kind of microscope. There was the click of a switch and the coin was outlined in light.

"A hundred-power magnifier I rigged up out of some discarded eyeglass lenses," he explained, looking into the eyepiece.

He began to shift the coin under the lens, mumbling to himself. Then he glanced up quickly.

Only he wasn't looking at me. He was looking right through me somewhere into outer space.

"What's wrong?" I asked excitedly. I knew the signs.

He raised his hand. "One moment," he said.

There was a puzzled frown on his face as he removed the coin from the magnifier. And then, without warning, he stuck out his tongue.

*And he licked the coin!*

"For Pete's sake! What gives?" I asked.

Brains put the coin under the magnifier again. He was talking fast to himself.

"Extraordinary! Most extraordinary!"

I was just about ready to pop a gasket when he beckoned to me.

"Jimmy, come over here and look at this."

I put my eye to the magnifier. There was the coin, huge and eerie like a strange planet. He had it placed so that the edge of the metal was in the center of the lens.

"Now observe closely," he said. "Is there anything special that you notice about the edge of the coin?"

I stared hard. Brains wasn't one for idle chatter. There must be something to notice or he wouldn't call my attention to it.

"Well, I see some fine scratches near the edge of the metal," I said uncertainly.

"And is there any special characteristic about those scratches?" he asked tensely.

"Well, they all run the same way."

I glanced up. There was a smile in the corner of his mouth.

"So what's so important about those scratches?" I asked.

"Those scratches are a clue. To a trained eye everything is a clue." He adjusted the magnifier, shifting the coin to another position.

"Now, this time observe the crack on the edge of the metal." I stared until my eyes began to water.

"That crack looks like an arrow cut through the metal, an arrow pointing toward the center of the coin," I said.

"Now look closely at the point of that arrow," Brains said. "Do you notice any cracks in the metal in that area?"

"None at all. That cut is sharp and clean. I can see some glints like silver down inside."

"Sharp observation, Jimmy," Brains said.

He clicked off the magnifier.

"All right," I said, "I'll bite! Those scratches on the edge of the coin—that crack in the metal—and the way you tasted the coin. What's the score?"

He smiled in that dry way our math teacher Mr. Cummings uses when he makes a complicated math problem look easy.

"Those scratches running the same way," Brains said casually, "are the marks made by emery paper to smooth the edge of the coin and give it a worn, aged look."

He let that sink in and then continued.

"And that cleft in the metal—if it were caused during the minting or when somebody dug a chisel into it, there'd be fine, hairline cracks at the narrowest point of the break, toward the center of the coin. No! That mark was engraved there, deliberately designed to look like a crack."

Maybe this all made sense to Brains. But I couldn't savvy what he was getting at.

"And why did you taste the coin?" I asked.

"I was testing the patina—the oxide on the coin. Such oxides are formed by the chemical action of salts in the atmosphere upon the metal. Oxides on ancient coins are always tasteless."

He paused for a long moment. "The patina on this coin is sharp and bitter to the tongue. I'd say it was nothing but a color varnish."

"Ye gads, you mean . . ." I began.

"Exactly! *That coin is an obvious fake!*"

"But Brains," I said, "it doesn't make sense. If the coin is a fake it can't be worth anything."

"Agreed!"

"Then why would the man with the black fingernail try to steal a worthless coin?"

"That's our next problem in the case, Operative Three," Brains said grimly. "To find the answer we must track down and unmask the mysterious man with the black fingernail."

Talk about famous last words. I could feel the icicles forming down my spine.

# 3 THE HUNT BEGINS

"Track him down?" I snorted. "Do you realize how many people live here in Crestwood and in Bleeker City?"

Brains stared at the ceiling. "As of the last census, exactly seventeen thousand, four hundred and thirty-eight in Crestwood. As for Bleeker City—"

"All right! All right!" I cut him off.

I might have known that human encyclopedia would have the exact figures at his fingertips.

"Look," I began again. "Seventeen thousand people in Crestwood alone. How do we go about finding the ones with black thumbnails? And when we find them, how will we know which one is our suspect?"

"By using our powers of deduction, Operative Three," said Brains, smiling patiently like a kindergarten teacher with a backward pupil. "Consider the facts. You must have acquired that counterfeit coin from one of your customers while you were making your newspaper collections this morning."

"Check," I said.

"Therefore, it is probable that the same customer would be most anxious to recover that coin."

I nodded. So far it made sense.

"Consequently," Brains went on, "our best procedure is to retrace your collection route and look for the customer with a black thumbnail."

I looked at him admiringly. Why couldn't I have figured it out as easily as that?

Suddenly, I had a chilling thought!

"What happens when we track this creep down? What if he starts some kind of fuss?"

"In our profession, Operative Three, there is always the element of danger," Brains replied grimly.

"That's just what I'm talking about," I blurted. "Why don't we just turn this whole affair over to the police?"

Brains stiffened. "As trained detectives, Benton and Carson are qualified to conduct their own criminal investigations. If the case should prove too difficult—then, and then only will we consult with the authorities."

"Well, it was only an idea," I said lamely.

He checked his watch. "It is now precisely eleven fifty-five," he said, raising his finger like the starting gun at a race track.

"Creeps! I've got to get home for lunch," I said. "Dad always has lunch with us on Saturdays. He doesn't like me to be late."

"Eleven fifty-five," repeated Brains, as if I hadn't even spoken. "If you eat with dispatch you should be back here by twelve-thirty."

The way that guy gave orders!

"All right! All right! I'll get going," I said.

"And when you report for duty again, please bring a list of the *Ledger* subscribers on your route," commanded Brains as I left.

He sounded so much like an army general that I wanted to salute.

I bicycled homeward, mad as a hornet. Brains had his gall

bossing me around. Wasn't I an equal partner in Benton and Carson?

Well, I'd take my own sweet time eating lunch. And I'd report for duty when I was good and ready.

Anyway, that's how I felt when I started home. But by the time I reached my house, four blocks away, I was having second thoughts on the subject.

Wasn't this *my* case? Wasn't *I* the one who'd discovered the mystery of the counterfeit coin?

If anyone was going to help solve it, it was going to be me. And when the man with the black thumbnail was tracked down, yours truly would be there to share the credit.

Mom was already serving lunch when I barged in. My sister Ann and my father were eating at the table as I came through the kitchen door.

My father frowned at me in disapproval. "Young man, will you ever be on time for your meals?" he said as I sat down.

"Yes, sir." I said, "But it wasn't my fault. You see . . ."

I'd just begun to explain—and then suddenly I stopped. My Dad works at the gas company. He's head accountant. He's a great guy, the best Dad a fellow ever had. But accountants aren't the kind of people you can talk to about mysterious coins and creepy strangers with black thumbnails.

So I kept quiet, mumbled something about how good the food was, and began to pack it away.

"I'm so glad you like it," said Ann.

For some reason my sister seemed to think something was funny. She was grinning from ear to ear.

I decided to play it cool. I finished my portion and then looked up.

"All right, Sis! What's so funny? Give me the punch line so I can laugh too."

Ann giggled. "I've got news for you. You just broke the world's record for downing chicken croquettes."

"*Chicken croquettes!*" I gulped.

If there was anything I hated in this wide world it was chicken croquettes! To me the stuff tasted like molded candle wax, warmed over.

I'd been in such a rush to get back to Brains, I never realized what I was eating.

"Ugh!" I said, pushing the plate aside. "I probably won't live through sundown."

"Probably not," Ann agreed, cheerfully. "You had an extra-large helping."

"How about some milk and pie?" asked my mother.

It was 12:25 by the kitchen clock.

"I'll settle for the milk," I said.

"No pie?" asked my father in disbelief. "You're sure you feel all right, son?"

"Topnotch, Dad. Just topnotch," I said.

I gulped down my milk, then hotfooted upstairs to my room. I grabbed the list of my newspaper subscribers from my desk and raced back to the kitchen and out the door.

I was riding my bike across the lawn toward the street when I heard the phone ring back in the house.

"Jimmy! For you!" called my mother, from the living room window. "It's Binky Barnes! He says it's important!"

Binky Barnes! At a time like *this!* Wouldn't you know? And of course it would be something important. *Everything* was important to Binky!

I told you before what a pest this kid was. No kidding, he had a built-in false alarm. His favorite hobby was making mountains out of molehills—like the time he came running home from Crescent Pond babbling about the footprints of a prehistoric reptile. He had half the kids in town hunting for a dinosaur until we found out those tracks were made by someone with swim-fins.

Or the time Binky found a genuine, pirate treasure chest out in the woods. Only it turned out to be someone's castoff trunk with a few pieces of broken costume jewelry inside.

"Tell Binky I've left," I called. "Tell him I've just blasted off for Mars!"

I didn't know what Binky had to tell me, but whatever it was, the story could wait. As a matter of fact, it could wait forever.

When I arrived at the Benton house, Brains was pacing the lab with all the patience of a caged jaguar.

"Operative Three," he commented acidly, "you are exactly three minutes late. I trust you have your list of *Daily Ledger* subscribers."

"Right here," I replied, handing it over.

He glanced down the page.

"There are quite a few names we can eliminate at once," he remarked.

We did.

First we crossed off the names of elderly folks who didn't get around much, like the Walshes and the Merriweathers. Then, the two clergymen on my list were ruled out. And since our mysterious culprit had obviously been a man, we penciled off the names of about two dozen female subscribers—like Miss Manley and Amanda Krock, the retired schoolteacher on Farnum Street.

"That leaves about seventy subscribers we have to see," Brains concluded. "Well, let us proceed with the investigation at once."

"Now hold on," I said. "How do we go about this? Do we just go up to my customers and say 'Good afternoon, Mr. Quackenbush. Turn over your hand. Do you mind if we examine your thumbnail, sir?' "

I thought that was a funny line, but it didn't get a laugh.

"Operative Three," Brains said, "while you were enjoying your lunch I was busy giving that problem considerable thought."

He regarded me reproachfully as if eating lunch was a capital crime.

"Here," he said, handing me a roll of paper tied with a ribbon.

I opened it. It was a hand-lettered scroll. My eyes popped as I read:

TO THE HONORABLE HENRY J. WORTHINGTON, MAYOR
*On the occasion of his sixtieth birthday, we, the under-*
*signed, present this testimonial as a token of our high*
*regard and esteem to the man who has devoted so many*
*years to the public service . . .*

It ran on in that kind of flowery language for another few lines. The bottom of the scroll had a lot of blank places for signatures.

I stared at Brains. "You losing your marbles? What's the mayor's birthday got to do with finding the man with the black thumbnail?"

"Elementary, my dear fellow," said Brains. "We need a good excuse to visit your subscribers and inspect their hands. What better way to accomplish that than to ask them to sign this testimonial scroll?"

See what I mean by Brains being smart? Man!

"Terrific!" I said admiringly. "And who did all that fancy lettering?"

"It *is* rather effective, isn't it?" said Brains. "I used my mother's lettering pens and colored inks."

If you remember, I told you his mother was an art teacher. You could see that Brains had inherited her talent. That scroll had the professional touch.

Brains rolled up his handiwork. "Come along," he said briskly. "We have much to accomplish before this day is over."

We slipped out of the garage and hopped on our bikes.

"Quiet now," warned Brains, "Mrs. Ray mustn't see us. She's certain to have some errand she wants done."

We'd slipped along the driveway past the Benton house and had just about reached the street when we heard the housekeeper's shrill voice calling after us.

"Barclay Benton! Come right back here this very moment! Barclay! It's important!"

Brains gasped, "Pretend you didn't hear her."

We rode like mad along Chestnut Drive and we didn't slow down until we'd covered five blocks.

"Brains," I said, trying to catch my breath, "maybe you should have gone back. It could be something important."

He grimaced. "If I know Mrs. Ray it was probably some paltry matter of absolute insignificance."

But that's where Brains was wrong. This time Mrs. Ray *did* have something important to say. And if we'd only stopped to listen we'd have saved ourselves a lot of trouble.

And brother, I do mean *trouble!*

# 4 DEAD END

"And now, Operative Three, let us proceed with the investigation," said Brains, in his deep official voice. "Our mission is to find the man with the black thumbnail."

*Creeps!* Did he *have* to remind me?

It was a warm April day, but I shivered as I remembered how that claw-like hand had crawled toward me across the wall of the telephone booth. Which one of my customers would it be? What would he do when we unmasked him? A guy like that might even be some dangerous kind of nut. He could even get violent!

But it was too late to turn back now. We were wheeling up to the door of the first subscriber on our list.

Brains' testimonial-scroll gimmick worked like a charm. Most people were glad to sign, so we got a good look at their thumbnails while they were using the pen.

But not everyone was friendly to the mayor of our fair city. Some of our citizens wanted to buy Worthington a one-way railroad ticket out of town. And a few suggested more economical ways of getting rid of him. Yipes, after what we learned about politics that day, I sure was glad I wasn't old enough to vote.

But by the time we'd spent two hours gathering signatures we still hadn't spotted what we were looking for—the suspect with the black thumbnail. True enough, we'd had a couple of exciting false alarms that had us jumping for a while.

Mr. Cripp, the mechanic at the Vine Street garage, had a black nail that looked mighty promising—until he wiped the grease off with an oil rag.

Then there was Mr. Ober, the baker on Clover Street. He was busy making pastry when we came in. His hands were covered with flour and he told us straight out he wouldn't bother washing them to sign anything for that faker Worthington.

But when Brains dumped some flour on the floor—accidentally of course—Mr. Ober had to clean it up. Naturally he had to wash his hands before he started making pastry again.

Yet all of Brains' conniving was a waste of time. Not one single black thumbnail!

And so it went. Before we knew it we were down to almost the bottom of our list. One of the names left was Mr. Peters. He lived on Balsam Street.

"Well, let's visit Mr. Peters next," said Brains.

"Now hold it," I said. "Old Horsey couldn't be our man in a million years!"

Horsey Peters was the principal of our school. The reason why everyone called him "Horsey" was—well, you just had to look at him to know.

Still, Mr. Peters was the last person to be mixed up in anything like this business of counterfeit coins.

"We cannot take anything for granted," Brains said.

So we headed up the Peters' walk and poked the front doorbell.

No answer.

"Probably no one home," I said hopefully. "Let's go, Brains."

I wanted to get out of there in a hurry. There was no sense

fooling around with the school principal if you could help it.

After Brains tried the bell again, and no dice, we struck across the Peters' lawn to get to our parked bikes. Suddenly Brains' head snapped around as if it were mounted on a spring.

I got the message! My partner had heard something back there in the rear of the Peters' garden.

Raising a finger to his lips for silence, Brains tiptoed around the side of the house. He beckoned me to follow.

I did, with my heart revving into high gear.

We'd reached a line of junipers when Brains stopped and pointed ahead. I pushed the prickly branches aside.

And there was Horsey Peters!

He was on his hands and knees, furtively scrabbling out a hole in the lawn about four feet from a line of rose bushes. Close beside him was a bulging burlap bag.

He must have sensed someone was watching him, because he whirled around and spotted us. If ever a man looked guilty and scared, it was old Horsey.

He jumped to his feet. "Ah, Barclay and James," he said with a nervous laugh. "What can I do for you boys?"

He was wearing oversized work gloves and he batted the loose earth from them.

Brains had spotted the gloves even before I had and he went into his spiel.

"Mr. Peters," he said, "we have this testimonial scroll for Mayor Worthington's birthday. And as one of the prominent citizens of our community . . ."

It was a pleasure to listen to an expert like Brains butter up his victim. He then held out a pen for Horsey's signature.

But it didn't work. Mr. Peters wasn't having any.

"I'm sorry, Barclay," he said. He'd forgotten about being scared. Right now he was looking downright peeved. "I'm afraid I can't sign that scroll. I wouldn't want the mayor to think I was trying to get in his good graces."

He said it apologetically, but we knew better. Everyone in

Crestwood had heard how Mayor Worthington had refused to sign a salary increase for Mr. Peters last year.

"And now, if you boys will excuse me, I have to—er—loosen up the soil around my roses," old Horsey said, and dismissed us with a nod.

But we didn't take the hint. We weren't going to leave until we'd seen his hands with those gloves *off!*

So far we hadn't found anyone with a black thumbnail. And right now Peters was suspect number *one!* And what's more, that burlap bag and the hole in the lawn looked mighty suspicious, too.

"Perhaps we can assist you, sir, in moving this bag," Brains said courteously.

Before Horsey could stop him, Brains reached out with his foot and nudged the burlap bag.

There was a clinking noise from inside.

I glanced at Brains sharply. Could that bag be filled with coins? *Counterfeit* coins?

"By the way, Mr. Peters, what's in that bag you're burying?" inquired Brains innocently.

It was a wild stab, but it hit dead center.

Poor old Horsey! From the way he winced you could see we had him dead to rights. Suddenly he braced himself as if he was about to walk the last mile.

"Boys," he said brokenly, "I'll make a clean breast of it—but you've got to promise not to tell anybody!"

Brother! My heart almost stopped as I waited for his confession.

"Mr. Peters, you may rely on our discretion," Brains assured him. "Our lips will be sealed. You'll probably feel better if you get it off your chest."

"You see," Horsey began, "there was this ugly old vase that my wife's favorite aunt gave us for an anniversary present. I was carrying it up to the attic to hide when I accidentally tripped and broke it."

He reached over and dumped a mess of broken pottery out of the burlap bag.

You should have seen those colors—orange, green, magenta—they had my eyes twitching. Old Horsey had done civilization a favor by breaking that vase.

Brains and I exchanged a look. There wasn't a color on those pieces of pottery to match the red on our faces.

"I was hoping to bury the pieces before Mrs. Peters came home," said Horsey, looking back over his shoulder nervously.

Horsey might be a big wheel around the school, but his wife sure had him buffaloed.

"By all means, Mr. Peters," said Brains as we started back toward the street. "It would be most advisable to do away with the evidence, at once."

"And don't worry," I assured him. "We didn't see a thing."

"Thanks, boys!" said Horsey. "By the way, as a token of my gratitude—hand me that pen, I'm ready to sign!"

"Sign what?" Brains and I blurted together.

"Why, that scroll for the mayor's birthday."

"Oh, the scroll," gulped Brains. He unrolled the parchment. "Of course, Mr. Peters! Happy to have your signature. Sign here, please!"

Horsey took off his gloves as he accepted the pen Brains offered him.

We had a good look at his fingers. He wasn't our man. Of course, that was obvious.

What was even more obvious was that we'd pulled one perfect, gold-plated, four-star, hand-embroidered goof.

We got out of there, but fast!

"You sure wasted a lot of fancy deducting," I said to Brains when we got back to our bikes. "Here we've just about finished the list of subscribers—and still no black thumbnail."

Brains bit his lips and consulted the frayed list. "Our next call is clearly the Barnes' domicile," he said.

"Don't bother," I told him. "It was *Mrs.* Barnes who paid me for the papers this week. Binky's Dad is out of town, so he couldn't be the man with the black thumbnail."

"I still think we ought to check," Brains said.

"O.K.," I said. "You go. Not me. After what we've been through I couldn't take that kid Binky and his whacky stories. As a matter of fact, he was trying to get me on the phone today . . ."

Suddenly a shrill voice echoed down the street—a voice that was midway between a screeching auto brake and a rusty gate.

"Jimmy! Hey, Jimmy Carson! Wait for me!"

I looked up to spot a towheaded kid hurtling toward us on a bicycle. "We're dead," I exclaimed. "It's Binky Barnes! We've got to hide somewhere!"

But it was too late. We were trapped! Binky was upon us!

"Jeepers!" puffed Binky as he hopped off his bike. "I've been chasing you all afternoon, Jimmy. I just missed you at your house."

Praise be! I thought to myself.

"Then I tried to reach you at the Bentons', but Mrs. Ray said you got away before she could stop you."

So that's why Mrs. Ray was calling us!

"All right," I said, "make it short! What is it *this* time? Did you see a flying submarine?"

"Very funny," said Binky indignantly. "But it just so happens that you've got something valuable that belongs to me."

I looked at him. "What, for Pete's sake?"

"My new Athenian drachma!" Binky said. "That's what!"

"Huh?" I gasped.

"His Athenian drachma," said Brains, dryly, and fished the mysterious coin out of his pocket.

"That's it!" Binky grabbed the silver piece in triumph. "My Mom gave it to you accidentally when she paid you for the papers this morning."

Brains sort of swayed. So did I. Talk about feeling let down! This was the *bottom!*

We'd been playing cloak and dagger up and down and across Crestwood trying to clear up the puzzle of the mysterious coin. And all the time the answer to the riddle had been following us around, trying to catch up with us!

"Well, that's that," I said. "The case has been solved!"

"You're so very wrong," Brains said quietly. "This case has just begun!"

# 5 SHADOWY TRAIL

"What do you mean, the case isn't solved?" I exclaimed. "We found out who that counterfeit coin belongs to, didn't we?"

"Ah, yes," replied Brains with that master-detective air of his. "But we still haven't uncovered the identity of the man with the black thumbnail. Nor have we unveiled the reason why he tried to steal the counterfeit drachma."

"Hold it!" interrupted Binky. "What's all this about my coin being a fake?"

We told him about my finding the drachma and about the man who tried to steal it and then discovering it was a fake.

"But it *can't* be a counterfeit," Binky protested when we finished. "You guys are just kidding."

"I'm sorry, Binky, but those are the facts," insisted Brains.

"Then that old geezer I bought it from gypped me out of twenty dollars," said Binky bitterly. "I saved that money for nearly a year—taking back deposit bottles to the store. Do you know how many bottles you have to find before you save twenty dollars?"

"Exactly four hundred at five cents apiece," commented Brains, offhandedly. "But your investment is safe. According to the legal statutes you are entitled to a full refund on the purchase price."

"That means you can get your money back on that imitation drachma," I translated for Binky.

Binky brightened up. "Hey! I'll head right down to the place where I bought it!"

"It's an old junk shop on Gorcey Street in Bleeker City," he went on. "A guy named Silas Gorme runs it."

"Bleeker City?" I blurted. The pieces of the jigsaw puzzle were beginning to fall into place. "Brains, this could tie in with the man who tried to steal the coin. Saffron's Drugstore is in Bleeker City too!"

"I think you have something there, Jimmy," Brains snapped. He turned to Binky. "That junk shop sounds like a most intriguing place. We'd like to accompany you when you return the coin."

"Well, okay! I don't mind company," Binky said. "The place is kind of creepy anyway. We could go there right now. It's only about three-thirty."

"Excellent," said Brains. "Just lead the way."

The fastest way to Bleeker City was by the Turnpike. So that's how we went. The authorities allow bikes on the Turnpike in our neck of the woods.

The junk shop in Bleeker City turned out to be in the shabbiest part of town. It was on the ground floor of a dilapidated, two-story frame building. The store windows were covered with grime. I could just about make out the lettering on the glass. It read:

## YE OLDE CURIO SHOPPE

Behind the dirty pane we could see a mess of old lamps, crockery, statues with clocks built into their stomachs, stuffed animals, and a lot of other castoff junk.

"Brother!" I said. "Do people actually buy this stuff?"

"There are many people who will buy anything," said Brains.

Binky flushed. "How did I know it was a fake? Look there." He pointed to a sign in a corner of the window.

*GENUINE GREEK DRACHMA*
2500 YEARS OLD

TAKE IT HOME FOR TWENTY DOLLARS

*A BARGAIN*

"A bargain!" I said. "It was a *steal!*"

"We may as well go in," said Brains. "Lead on, Jimmy."

The door of the shop was recessed on one side of the display window. I was about to open it when I froze.

Hanging in the window, within inches of my face, was a tiny, brown, human head about the size of a baseball!

Till the end of my life I'll remember it, dangling there by a hank of stringy black hair, its eyes and lips sewn shut with leather lacing.

Creeps! I could feel my hair curl into a permanent wave.

"What's *that?*" I gasped, trying to catch my breath.

"Oh, it's one of those shrunken heads imported from South America," said Binky cheerfully.

"Perhaps you're right," commented Brains, with scientific detachment. "But I understand some excellent plastic imitations are being manufactured right here in this country. Just open the door. There's nothing to worry about."

Nothing to worry about! Ha! How did Brains know for sure this thing was made of plastic? It *could* be the real thing, imported from the South American jungle.

Creeps! For all I knew maybe that shrunken head was made right here in this shop!

I forced myself to open the door. It swung wide with a loud, slow creak—like the main entrance of a haunted house.

"Proceed, Jimmy. We're right behind you," Brains directed.

I stepped back.

"After you," I murmured politely.

Brains shot me a poisonous look and stepped through into the store with Binky behind him.

Operative Three followed . . . slowly . . .

It was like stepping into a dark and moldy cave. I wouldn't have been surprised to see bats flying out at us.

From somewhere in the back of the shop came a tapping sound, and the ring of metal striking metal. Then, in a distant corner, I saw the shadow of a man stirring against a faint blur of light.

"Creeps! What's he making back there?" I whispered.

"More shrunken heads, maybe," said Binky cheerfully.

I dug my elbow into his ribs. That joke wasn't very funny.

Abruptly, the tapping sound stopped. I looked back into the darkness. The faint light had vanished. Suddenly the piles of junk seemed to be closing in on us—the silence was so thick you could cut it with a knife.

"Where—where'd he go?" I croaked, backing up against Brains.

Binky was crowding Brains from the other side. "Jeepers," Binky hissed, "I never realized what a spooky place this was."

Suddenly a voice spoke behind us.

"What do you kids want here?"

We whirled.

Looming over us was a scowling, unshaven face with two beady eyes—a man with the bald head, scrawny neck and huge nose-beak of a vulture!

And in his hand he held a hammer!

*Creeps!*

# 6 TRACKDOWN

It was Binky who finally spoke up. "It's about this coin, Mr. Gorme." He held out the drachma. Or he tried to. Because his hand shook so hard he dropped it on the floor.

Brains picked it up.

"What about the coin?" growled the man Binky had called Gorme.

"It's counterfeit," Brains said. His voice quavered a little.

Gorme's eyes narrowed. "Now what's a kid like you know about counterfeit?" he rasped, as he shoved his face down toward Brains.

"It so happens that I have examined this coin with the finest scientific optical devices," said Brains. "And I am ready to make an affidavit that it is not genuine."

Gorme backed off and changed his tone.

"Well, okay," he said grudgingly. "If you say it's a fake, I'll take your word for it."

He pulled aside the apron he was wearing and extracted a thick, oily-looking roll of bills.

"I don't want any trouble. Suppose I give you back your money—and we forget the whole thing, hey?"

As he peeled a twenty off the roll, I gasped! Not at the size of the wad—but because Silas Gorme was wearing a black finger guard—and it was on his *left thumb!*

I turned to give Brains the tip-off. He looked right back at me and shook his head.

He'd seen that thumb guard too, and he was warning me to keep my lip buttoned.

"All right," Gorme was saying to Brains. "Let's have the coin, kid." He held out the twenty.

But Brains wasn't having any.

"I'm sorry, sir, but I don't think the money alone will be enough."

"But Brains . . ." interrupted Binky, as he saw his money go glimmering down the drain.

Brains didn't even hear him. "You see, Mr. Gorme, we're far more interested in finding out where that bogus coin came from. As public-spirited citizens, our main task should be to find out where that coin was minted—and by whom."

Gorme's neck seemed to swell up. He looked even more like a vulture now.

"Where I got that silver piece is none of your business! Just hand it over and beat it," he growled.

"Now, now! There's no point in losing your temper, Mr. Gorme," said Brains patiently."All we ask is some information which you, as an honest citizen—"

Suddenly I noticed that Brains was carelessly holding the coin just a few inches from Gorme's left hand.

And Gorme had noticed Brains' carelessness too. His muscles tensed. I knew he was going to grab for that drachma.

"Brains! Watch it!" I yelled.

I was too late. Gorme's hand was already moving like a striking snake.

But Brains was way ahead of him. He yanked the coin out of

reach just in time. And Gorme's open hand rammed against a secondhand dresser standing close by.

"My hand!" roared Gorme, his face twisting in pain as he went into a war dance.

He said a few other things, too, which I won't repeat here.

"My blasted thumb," moaned Gorme. "I've hurt it again."

It was only then that I realized Gorme had injured the hand with the thumb guard. As he yanked at the laces of the plastic sleeve I sneaked a look at Brains. There was the ghost of a smile around his lips.

My foxy, redheaded friend had baited Gorme into slamming that masked thumb.

And the trick had worked.

I stood there holding my breath, watching Gorme opening the laces.

When the guard came off, Brains and I were speechless.

We'd tracked him down at last—the man with the black thumbnail!

It was Silas Gorme!

# 7 THE THIRD DEGREE

As I watched Gorme favor his hand, I shivered. I could still remember how that hairy claw scuttled past my eyes back there in the telephone booth of Saffron's Drugstore.

Well, we caught up with our chief suspect. But what *now?*

There were still a dozen pieces of the jigsaw puzzle that refused to fit together.

Why had Silas Gorme been so anxious to recover the counterfeit? Why wouldn't he reveal where the coin came from? Who was he protecting? And why?

Asking questions was easy. Getting the answers out of Gorme would be quite a problem.

But Brains was already working on it.

"I regret the injury to your thumb, Mr. Gorme," Brains was saying. "I trust it will be better by the time we return with the police."

"You mean you're going to the police with that coin?" Gorme said. "All they can do is make me give you back your money. So why not be smart, and . . ."

Gorme had something there. There was nothing else the police could do for us, I thought. I should have figured Brains had another angle.

"I'm afraid you don't realize all the aspects of this case," he said severely. "We also intend to notify the police that you, Silas Gorme, are guilty of attempted larceny."

"Attempted larceny!" Gorme paled. "What do you mean?"

Brains turned on him accusingly. "You are the culprit who tried to snatch this drachma from Jimmy here in Saffron's Drugstore this morning."

Brains pointed accusingly at Gorme's injured thumb. "The man who tried to steal that coin had a blackened thumbnail *exactly* like yours."

"That doesn't prove a thing," snarled Gorme defiantly. "I wasn't in that store today."

Brains was pressing him hard but Gorme wasn't ready to surrender. I saw a way to help. It was a long shot, but I tried it.

"Why, Mr. Gorme, how can you say that?" I said. "I saw you in Saffron's myself. You were in the next telephone booth."

Gorme was desperate now. "It's a lie!" he shouted. "No one could have seen me! I had my back turned and—"

He stopped dead without bothering to finish.

He'd opened his mouth too wide, and shoved his foot right in.

"So you *were* in Saffron's Drugstore?" snapped Brains. "Why?"

Gorme was a different man, now that we had him hooked. He was scared stiff and was ready to talk.

"I had to telephone a customer," he said. "You see I don't have a phone here in the store. While I was making my call I overheard someone in the next booth. Whoever it was sounded like a detective reporting into headquarters. He kept calling himself Operative Three. He was talking to his chief about a mysterious coin that was going to be investigated."

Get that! I'd sounded like a *real detective!*

Gorme took out a grimy handkerchief and wiped his brow nervously. "From the conversation I realized they were discussing the drachma I'd sold to this kid here. I was afraid I was in in for trouble with the law—"

"And so . . ." needled Brains, riding him hard.

"And so I guess I kind of lost my head, reached into the phone booth and tried to snatch the coin."

Gorme finished the story. I caught sight of Binky sitting there listening in with his mouth wide open and his eyes almost popping.

Heck! I'd bet this was wilder than any story he ever invented.

"Well," said Brains, as Gorme's confession ended. "No matter what your motive, it was still attempted larceny. Unless you tell us where you obtained this spurious drachma, I will be forced to go to the police for assistance."

For a minute Gorme looked daggers at Brains, and then, suddenly, he smiled. He reminded me of one of those lizards that can change his colors at will.

"You win, son! I know when I'm licked. I'll tell you where I got it."

He paused. I could see his brain working like a calculating machine figuring his next move.

"Matter of fact," Gorme continued with sudden indignation, "I'll take you to the scoundrel myself! Why should I protect the guy who got me into all this trouble? He had his gall selling me that counterfeit. And I won't take the blame for it. I've got my reputation to think about."

Gorme took off his apron. "Wait here a moment, boys. I'll slip on my jacket and take you to him right now."

As he disappeared into the gloom at the rear of the shop, I whispered my congratulations to Brains. "Good work. You cracked him wide open!"

Brains didn't appear too triumphant. "I'm not so sure Silas Gorme told us the whole truth," he said. "After all, he didn't talk up until we threatened to go to the police."

"You mean he's still hiding something from us?"

Brains shrugged and let it go at that.

I looked around for Silas Gorme. It sure was taking him a long time to put on his jacket. Then, abruptly, he came toward us.

We followed him out of his shop into the street. Gorme was smiling, of all things. It put me on my guard. We'd caught this man lying. We'd caught him trying to steal!

Creeps! What would he try next?

We'd have to keep a mighty sharp eye on Mr. Silas Gorme!

# 8  INCRIMINATING EVIDENCE

But to my surprise Gorme didn't give us any more trouble. He led the way out of the shabby part of town to where Gorcey Street hit Broadway—the shopping center of Bleeker City. We followed close behind him, wheeling our bikes along the curb.

At Broadway, Gorme turned left and headed along the walk crowded with last-minute week-end shoppers. Then he stopped near a small store.

On the window of the shop was the neatly lettered sign reading:

BLEEKER CITY

COIN AND STAMP EXCHANGE

Jeremy Dexter, PROP.

"This is it," Gorme said, indicating the store with his thumb. We hopped our bikes up on the walk and leaned them on the building.

The windows of the store were crowded with sets of stamps and coins. Poor Binky's mouth was watering as he goggled at the display. But this wasn't any time for window shopping. Silas Gorme had the door open and was beckoning us to follow him inside.

We did.

The store was a bright, cheery place. Sets of stamps and coins were arranged in freshly painted glass cases and on shelves. Seated at a desk in the rear was a man with iron-gray hair and glasses. He'd been examining some stamps under a magnifying glass and as he came toward us I saw that he was short and quite pale. His clothes hung on him like a loose sack and I got the idea that he'd lost a lot of weight lately.

"Good afternoon, Mr. Gorme," he said to Silas. I was surprised to hear his voice. It was bright, almost youthful.

Then he turned and smiled at us. "And are these gentlemen with you?"

That gentlemen bit didn't fool me at all. If this guy thought he could butter us up, he had another think coming.

"Yeah! They're with me, Dexter," said Gorme. He turned to Brains. "Okay, kid, show him the coin!"

Brains still had the drachma in his pocket. Now he fished it out and handed it to Dexter.

The storekeeper pulled his eyeglasses far down on his nose and examined the coin.

His face lit up with a cheery smile. "Ah, yes! The Greek drachma I sold you a month ago."

Brains flashed me a half-surprised look. Then Gorme wasn't lying. He *had* bought it here.

"A splendid specimen, even if it is a bit worn," commented Jeremy Dexter admiringly.

"Splendid specimen!" exploded Silas. "Why that thing is an out-and-out fake! You had your nerve palming that off on me!"

Dexter flushed. All of a sudden his hand was shaking. From the way he bit his lips, he was fighting to keep calm.

"Mr. Gorme, what you say is incredible," he said. "Will you permit me to examine this coin more carefully?"

"Examine it all you like. It's still a fake," sneered Gorme.

Dexter took the drachma back to his desk. There, under a bright light, he checked the drachma with a large magnifying glass.

"Watch Dexter closely," Brains warned with his lips close to my ear. "He might try a switch!"

He didn't have to tell me that. I'd played enough T-formation football to watch out for any razzle-dazzle.

Just the same I sneaked a look at Silas Gorme, too. He was standing behind me, frowning as he examined a set of gaudy stamps in a display case. He must have touched something dusty, because he was wiping his hands on a handkerchief. He was stuffing the handkerchief back into his pocket when I turned my attention back to Jeremy Dexter.

Suddenly Dexter stood erect and came over. He kept frowning at the coin in his hand as if something puzzled him.

"This is most confusing, Mr. Gorme," said Dexter. "This coin is definitely a counterfeit. But it is most certainly *not* the specimen I sold you."

"Now just a minute. I bought that coin right here in this shop," growled Silas. "I took your word that it was genuine. Then, last week, I sold it to this boy here."

He jerked a thumb at Binky. Binky straightened up and tried to look important.

"That's right," Binky said. "I paid Mr. Gorme twenty dollars for that coin, my whole life savings!"

"Twenty dollars?" asked Dexter, distressed. "But Mr. Gorme, you paid *twenty-five* for that drachma."

"What's that to you?" bellowed Silas. "I needed the money, so I sold it at a loss! Is that a crime?"

"Not at all, sir." I could see that Dexter was going into a slow boil. "For all that coin is worth, you should have given it away for nothing."

"I've had just about enough of this, Dexter," snarled Gorme. "Just hand over that twenty-five dollars you cheated me out of."

That did it! Dexter slammed the drachma down on a case.

"How dare you make such an accusation? I examine every item on sale here. The drachma I sold you was genuine! Where you got this shabby imitation is none of my affair."

Brains and I exchanged puzzled looks. *Somebody* was lying. But *who?*

By now Gorme was in a rage. "Dexter, you're a dirty little cheat," he shouted, yanking open the street door. "You've had your chance to return my money. Now, I'm going to call in the law!"

With that he charged out into the street.

Dexter was the color of a bed sheet. He took a small bottle from his pocket, uncapped it and shook a tiny pill into his palm. Then he popped the pill into his mouth and swallowed. Right then I knew that Jeremy Dexter was a mighty sick man.

I yanked Brains' arm. "Looks like the pot's going to boil over in here. Maybe we'd better beat it before the police come."

"Too late to worry about that, Jimmy," replied Brains, nodding toward the front window.

Through the plate glass I saw Gorme and a beefy-looking policeman in a blue uniform pushing through the crowd that was beginning to gather outside the store.

"Right in here, Officer Burney!" said Gorme, leading the man in blue through the door.

He pointed an accusing finger at Dexter, who was leaning on a display case for support. "That's him, the swindler! He sold me a counterfeit coin and now he won't return my money."

Burney hauled a small leather notebook out of his pocket. "All right now, tell it to me slowly," he said. "What's the story—and make it short!"

Briefly Silas gave him the details. I noticed that he skipped the part about trying to snatch the coin from me in Saffron's phone booth. Since that wasn't important I let it slide.

As Burney closed his notebook he turned toward Brains and me. "I understand why that Barnes kid is here. But where do you two fit in?"

"Well, you see," I began eagerly—

I was just about to tell him that Brains and I were the private investigators whose remarkable sleuthing had cracked this case wide open, and that if he needed any advice we'd be glad to help him—when all of a sudden I felt Brains' bony elbow ram into my ribs.

"Allow me to explain, Officer," said Brains, interrupting smoothly. "We are Binky's friends, and we came along to see justice done."

"Great! Great! The more the merrier," commented Officer Burney sarcastically.

He turned to Gorme. "Mr. Gorme, it seems to be your word against Mr. Dexter's."

"That's not the question, Officer!" ranted Gorme. "Dexter admits selling me the coin. And he admits it's a counterfeit!"

Burney scratched his head. He picked up the coin and held it to the light. "Now, how do you know for sure this thing is a fake?"

"Here, let me show you," said Gorme irritably.

Gorme had been pacing the length of the store nervously. Now he stepped toward the policeman.

Suddenly there was a loud thump! Gorme let out a wild yell and grabbed at his knee.

"That drawer!" he bawled. "Dexter, why don't you keep your blasted shop in order?"

We looked. Beneath a display case was an open drawer. It extended into the aisle for about six or eight inches.

It was obvious that Gorme had slammed his leg against it in passing.

"I'll close it, sir," said Brains. He had his hand on the drawer, about to push it shut when all at once he stopped and stared!

"Most interesting," Brains said in his best Sherlock Holmes

voice. He reached down into the drawer and came up with two short, round bars of metal.

The police officer grimaced. "So what's interesting about a couple of chunks of steel, son?"

"Kindly observe the ends of these metal bars," said Brains.

He held the ends of the bars tilted toward the light. Everyone crowded around to see what he was getting at. I noticed it first. The smaller ends of both metal cones were carved into a design.

One bar was engraved with the image of a popeyed owl— and beside it were the letters AOE in reverse. The other bar carried a reverse head of Athena, wearing a helmet.

"Brains," I gasped. "This design is just like the engraving on that coin, except that it's backward!"

"Exactly," said Brains. "If Officer Burney will let me have the disputed drachma, I would like to perform an experiment."

Burney's mouth was hanging open. Without another word he handed Brains the coin.

Carefully Brains laid the drachma in the hollow design carved in the steel. It nestled perfectly.

"Gentlemen," said Brains quietly, "if I am not mistaken these are the dies which were used to mint the counterfeit coin."

Talk about dropping a bomb! We all stared at those dies as if we were shell-shocked.

"What did I tell you?" gloated Silas. "There's all the proof you need, Officer. The coin was faked right here in this store."

That pill hadn't helped Dexter much. He was shaking like a leaf, staring at the dies as if he couldn't believe what he saw.

"Incredible!" he was muttering. "Where did those dies come from?"

If this was an act, Dexter was the greatest actor in the world. But he didn't have a chance. He'd been caught with the goods.

"Daddy! Daddy!" called a voice behind me.

The front door slammed open and a tornado in a plaid shirt and jeans blasted past me toward Dexter.

It was a kid of about ten. He was wearing a baseball cap and

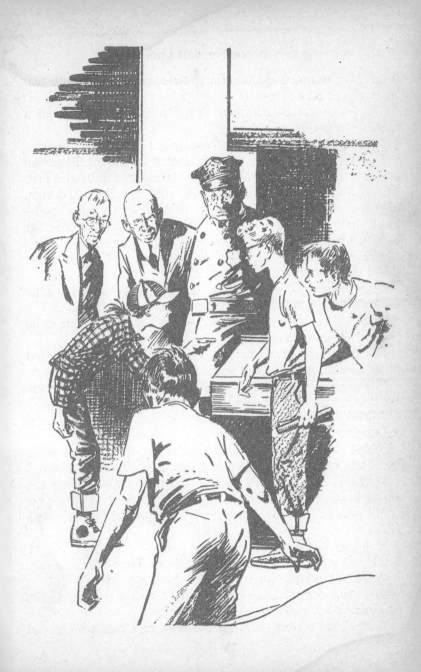

he kept pulling at Dexter's arm. "Daddy, are you all right? You're not having one of your attacks, are you?"

"Everything's all right, Terry," said Dexter, trying to calm the kid down. "We were just having a little discussion."

But Terry didn't seem to believe a word of it. The kid whirled around to face us. "What's going on here? What have you people done to my Dad? He's a sick man! He's not allowed to get excited!"

Brains and I exchanged glances. Usually both of us had plenty to say, but not right then. How do you tell a kid his father's been caught red-handed in a crooked scheme? Even Binky stood there with his mouth closed, and for Binky that wasn't easy, believe me!

It was Officer Burney who spoke first. "We've had a little trouble here, Terry."

"I'll say," growled Silas Gorme. "We just caught your father in a counterfeiting scheme."

"That's a lie!" Terry snapped. "Dad wouldn't do a thing like that. You couldn't prove it in a million years."

"Couldn't we?" sneered Gorme. He pointed to the dies in the policeman's hand. "Those are the very dies your father used to make the counterfeit. He would have gotten away with it, too, if not for that young man over there." Gorme nodded toward Brains.

At that particular moment Brains looked as if he wanted to crawl into a hole and hide.

Terry stepped up to him angrily.

"Now wait a minute," said Brains, almost stuttering. "I just happened to look in an open drawer when I spotted those dies —so naturally—"

"So you just *happened* to look in that drawer?" exploded Terry. "Why you nosy snooper!"

With that he balled up a fist and swung from the floor.

That punch would have knocked Brains for a loop if it had landed. But it didn't, because Brains ducked. And who do you think was standing right behind Brains at the time? You guessed it. Old faithful Operative Three! And when Brains dodged, I caught that fist, right in the face! And down I went!

I bounced up fighting mad. "Let me at that skinny runt! I'll tear him apart," I was yelling.

But Burney was holding me by the scruff of the neck. And Brains was yelling, "Relax, Jimmy! Hold it! You can't hit him!"

"Why not?" I bellowed.

"Because he's a *she!* Take a good look," said Brains.

I did! And I nearly keeled over.

Terry Dexter's baseball cap had fallen off. The kid was wearing a short ponytail hairdo.

"If she's a girl, why's her name Terry?" I growled suspiciously.

"It's my nickname," snapped Terry. "My full name's Theresa! And even if I *am* a girl, I can lick you . . . and all your friends, too." Her jaw jutted out like a bull terrier spoiling for a fight.

"Here," interrupted Burney, taking Terry by the arm, "there'll be no more of *that!* There's been enough arguing and fighting in here already."

Burney pushed his notebook back under his tunic. "All this is too much for me. I'm afraid we'll all have to go down to see Judge Parker at Town Hall."

"Are you arresting me, Officer?" asked Dexter. He had his hand on Terry's shoulder, sort of leaning on her.

"Not if I can help it, Mr. Dexter," replied Burney. "But there's been a disturbance of the peace here, and there's a suspicion of a crime."

"What about us?" asked Binky, looking scared. "It's all right if we go home now, isn't it?" By now he was wishing he'd never seen that crummy drachma.

"Sorry, boys, but you're included in the invitation too. You're witnesses, and as good citizens you'd better come along and tell the judge whatever you know."

So, minutes later, there we were, wheeling our bikes down Broadway toward Town Hall with half of Bleeker City's population gawking at us. Brother! How did we get into this mess?

"Jeepers," whispered Binky, "are you sure we're not being arrested?"

"Don't be ridiculous, Binky," said Brains. "We haven't committed any crime!"

But I wasn't so sure of that. Maybe we'd done something wrong after all. Maybe this Judge Parker wouldn't like the idea of kids playing detective and solving mysteries. Maybe he was the kind of grownup that didn't like kids at all!

Creeps! He might toss the three of us in the clink and throw away the key!

# 9  SHADOWED

But I was dead wrong about Judge Parker. He proved to be a gray-haired old fellow with a kindly smile. You got the idea that he was probably a swell grandfather to some lucky kid.

He listened closely to Officer Burney's report, asked Gorme and Dexter a few questions, then adjusted his glasses and spoke down to Dexter, who was standing with the other grownups in front of the bench.

"Mr. Dexter," he said, "ordinarily the simple sale of spurious coins does not necessarily prove a felony or misdemeanor."

"For goodness' sake, why doesn't he talk English," I whispered to Brains. He was seated between Binky and me in the front row of seats.

"Quiet," hissed Brains, "or the judge will find you in contempt of court!"

I clammed up fast.

The judge kept talking, using fancy words like "manufacturing fraudulent articles for sale," "conspiracy" and "defrauding the public."

I couldn't make it all out, but I could see that finding those dies in his store really put the finger on Jeremy Dexter.

"Under the circumstances," concluded the judge, "I'll have to direct you to appear before the Grand Jury for examination, Mr. Dexter."

Dexter started to shake again. But he steadied down when the judge added that since he was a businessman in the community the court wouldn't ask any bail and that he was releasing Dexter in his own custody for the present.

Dexter thanked him and sat down in a corner. But I noticed the worried look on Terry's face as her father popped another pill into his mouth.

I thought it was over, but then the judge rapped with his gavel and called Silas Gorme up to the bench and told him to pay Binky his twenty dollars.

Gorme was burned up, but Judge Parker laid down the law. He said Binky's deal had been with *Gorme* and that Silas would have to make the refund then and there!

Believe me, it all caught Binky by surprise. He never expected to see that money again. He walked up to the bench trying to act dignified—but he was about as dignified as a bouncing India-rubber ball.

Anyway, once Gorme handed over the twenty the judge rapped with his gavel again, and we were headed out to the street.

Brother, was I glad that was over!

Silas Gorme was right behind us when we reached the sidewalk. He shot us a dirty look. I could see that twenty would be on his mind for a long time.

We were climbing on our bikes when Terry and her father came out of Town Hall. Mr. Dexter looked whiter than ever, but he sort of nodded our way. To show us there were no hard feelings, I guess.

But that kid Terry just clenched her fists and glared angrily at us.

"Brother," said Binky nervously, "that Terry's just aching to take us on—one at a time, or all three of us together. And she doesn't care which."

"You're right, Binky. That girl is definitely contemplating assault and battery," Brains agreed. "I would recommend that we leave Bleeker City immediately."

"Second the motion," I said.

There was no vote. We just scooted for the town limits.

All the way back to Crestwood, Binky kept racing ahead and then turning back to wait for us impatiently. "What's holding up you guys?" he complained. "Boy! I can't wait till I tell the kids what happened today!"

"I can see it all now," I remarked to Brains. "By the time Binky gets done embroidering the story, he'll have us fighting a pitched battle with a gang of armed bank robbers."

Brains frowned. "Binky, I suggest you keep all the details of this case strictly confidential. After all, we won't know if Mr. Dexter is a counterfeiter until a jury decides. We do want to be fair!"

"Well, yeah. We want to be fair all right," admitted Binky, reluctantly.

Binky wasn't completely convinced, but he'd always admired Brains Benton. And after today's events, Brains was his number one hero and the fountain of all wisdom.

Anything Brains said was O.K. with Binky—especially since it was because of his efforts that Binky got back his twenty dollars.

"Okay," said Binky, "my lips are sealed. But believe me, it won't be easy."

With that settled, Binky raced ahead, leaving us far behind —which was fine with me.

Now that we were alone, I had a bone to pick with Brains.

"What did you mean when you said we didn't know whether or not Jeremy Dexter was a counterfeiter? Didn't we practically catch him red-handed with those dies?"

"Those dies are just what make me so skeptical of the entire case against Dexter," Brains said.

That jolted me! I almost forgot to turn off at the Crestwood exit of the Turnpike.

Brains continued. "It seems to me that anyone clever enough to be a counterfeiter would be far too cunning to hide those dies where any customer might accidentally find them."

Good gravy! He really had something there!

"And another peculiar thing," Brains went on. "That open drawer projected into the main aisle of the shop, yet no one stumbled over it until the police officer was present to see the incriminating evidence."

"But Brains," I protested, "it was *you* who discovered those dies in the drawer."

"True," he agreed. "But I believe that someone pulled the drawer open and planted those dies just before Officer Burney entered the store."

That hit me so hard I braked to a sudden stop. Luckily I was right in front of our house on Maple Street. Brains stopped beside me.

"Planted the dies?" I exploded. "Who could have done that? I know it wasn't me—or you—or Binky! And if Mr. Dexter didn't put them there, it leaves only . . ."

"Precisely," said Brains tersely. "That leaves only Silas Gorme!"

"Then you think we sent the wrong man to jail?" I asked. Even the thought made me feel sick.

"Dexter isn't in jail yet," Brains pointed out. "If we pursue our investigation a bit further, we may find some more evidence before the case comes to trial."

Brains mounted his bike again. "Well, good-bye for now, Operative Three. I'll be in touch with you tomorrow. I want to ponder what facts we have in this case, and then we'll make our plans."

"Tomorrow's Sunday," I reminded him. "And after church,

I promised my Dad I'd stay home and catch up with my math."

"Hm," replied Brains, a little ruffled because I'd interfered with his plan. "Well, then, I'll use the time to continue some new experiments in infra-red photography. . . . However, should there be any important developments, call me at once."

With that he rode away.

Important developments! Ha! Nothing *ever* happened in Crestwood on a Sunday. But brother! Was I about to be proven wrong!

I went to sleep that night all wound up and worried about Jeremy Dexter, and whether I had helped to send an innocent man to prison. It took me hours to fall asleep.

Then, long before dawn, I was awakened by a violent thunderstorm. So I spent the second half of the night tossing and turning and worrying some more.

By morning the rain was over, but now a gloomy fog blotted out everything more than fifty feet away.

That fog didn't cheer me up at all.

And when we got to church I could see this just wasn't going to be my day. The sermon was on the subject of the Ninth Commandment: THOU SHALT NOT BEAR FALSE WITNESS.

It could have been my imagination, but I'd swear our minister was looking straight at *me* all the time he spoke.

By the time we got home, I had an advanced case of the galloping jitters. I pretended to eat lunch heartily, hoping the folks wouldn't notice how I felt. They didn't. But every mouthful I took seemed to stick in my throat, I was that jumpy.

Mother and Dad had a date for an afternoon visit with some friends, and they got started right after lunch. My sister Ann had a meeting of the Junior Dramatic Society and she left after washing the lunch dishes.

That left yours truly all alone in the house. And what with that creepy fog outside the window and me with the jitters, brother, I was just about ready to pop.

I tackled my math book in sheer self-defense. I had been

grinding away at theorems and axioms for about an hour, when out of the clear blue I got a sort of crawling sensation along the back of my neck.

*I was being watched!*

I could almost feel someone's eyes drilling into my back. Just the thought of it was enough to turn my spine into one long chain of ice cubes.

I sat there without moving, trying to figure it out. I was alone in the house. If anyone was watching me, it had to be through one of the windows.

I whirled in my seat—*Creeps!* I nearly collapsed! Something slid away from the window right behind me. It could have been a face, a hand, a head—but it ducked too fast for me to make it out.

But somebody was shadowing me, that I knew!

It took all the nerve I had, but I forced myself to look out of the window.

There was no one in sight. I couldn't see anything but billows of fog drifting across the lawn. The mist was so thick I could just about make out the trees and hedge on our property line only fifty feet away.

Carson, I told myself, you'll be seeing little pink elephants next. Keep it up and you'll be getting a social call from the men in white coats.

I was just beginning to talk myself into it. The butterflies in my stomach were coming in for a landing, when suddenly I saw a shadow slip behind the twisted old oak tree at the far side of the lawn.

One look at that moving shadow and those butterflies zoomed off for the wild blue yonder again.

I was in a panic. Who was lurking out there? What did he want? Why was he spying on me? Whoever it was was up to some dirty work or he wouldn't be slinking around like that.

Ten to one he had a weapon and was just looking for a chance to finish me off.

Every minute counted! I shot through the doorway into the hall. I grabbed for the phone. It slipped from my fingers, but I managed to catch it before it hit the floor. Then I was dialing the Benton number.

Maybe I could get through to X with a final message before the end came.

# 10 THE FACE IN THE FOG

I heard the phone ringing at the other end. If that gabby Mrs. Ray picked up the receiver, I might be a dead duck before I could get through to Brains.

But the breaks were with me. It was Brains who answered.

"Brains! Out there in the yard!" I gabbled. "Someone's sneaking around! Spying on me! They're out to get me! You've got to do something, I tell you!"

"Relax, Operative Three," Brains said. "Try to calm down and give me the facts."

"Calm down?" I yelled. "That's easy for *you* to say! You're not being shadowed. Nobody's sneaking around *your* house with a gun, trying to finish you off."

Brains suddenly sounded anxious. "Did you see anyone with a gun?"

"Well, no," I sputtered. "But I just know he's armed and is waiting to finish me off. I'm getting out of here before he breaks in."

"Don't leave the house," cautioned Brains. "This prowler may be the man behind the counterfeiting scheme. He realizes that you are an important witness in the case. He may be there to eliminate you."

*Eliminate me?* What a thing to say at a time like this!

"Now listen," Brains said urgently. "I've just evolved an excellent plan of operations. That tool shed in the back yard of your house, at the end of the driveway, is it locked?"

"No!" I said. "But if you think I'm going to risk my life to sneak out there and hide—"

Brains cut me off. "Jimmy, I think we've got a chance to trap the prowler!"

I'd just as soon try to trap an atom bomb! My stomach was in knots just at the thought of it.

"Leave it all to me," Brains was saying excitedly. "Just stay where you are. Keep the light on and pretend to be studying. Act nonchalant. I'll be over in a matter of minutes."

"For Pete's sake, hurry!" I blurted. "And Brains—if I'm dead when you get here . . ."

"Oh, don't be an idiot," he snapped.

There was a click and the line went dead.

I hung up. Believe me, if I could have crawled through that phone to Brains' house and safety, I would have done it.

Back in the living room, I got hold of myself. Act nonchalant, Brains had said. All right, I'd try it his way. But I couldn't keep my eyes away from the window. I kept sneaking looks out into the fog, trying to spot the intruder.

But when I did, was I sorry! He was hiding behind the hedge and staring right down my throat with a big pair of binoculars! I ducked away and hugged the wall. *Brother!*

I sat down and stared into my math book, but my mind was racing like mad.

What was that prowler doing out there in the fog? Was he closing in? Where was Brains?

Maybe I shouldn't wait for Brains. Maybe I ought to call the police.

It was right about then that I heard the back door close. I came out of my chair like a bouncing ball.

This was it! Somebody had come through the back door into the kitchen.

Well, that did it!

No big gorilla could barge into *my* house just like that. I grabbed a small vase from the piano. It wasn't much, but it would have to do. I gripped it by the neck and tiptoed down the hall.

Yes! I could hear somebody moving around in the kitchen. The big thug was preparing to ambush me. I hefted the vase. This could be my finish, but I'd go down fighting.

I shoved through the kitchen door ready for a battle royal. When I saw who was there I nearly collapsed.

It was Brains Benton!

"Still with us, Operative Three?" he inquired.

You could see my pal Brains was a great tonic for the nerves in a pinch like this.

"Brother," I whispered. "You don't know how close you came to being crowned just now. As a matter of fact I'm still tempted to let you have it. What took you so long?"

"I've been around for the past ten minutes," Brains added as he placed a small plastic box on the table. "I came across Dr. Masters' property at the back of your house. I've been working in the tool shed."

"For Pete's sake! What were you doing out *there?*" I whispered.

"Setting a trap for the prowler," Brains replied. He was working on the plastic box now.

"Trap? How can you trap that guy with a plastic box?"

"Patience, Operative Three," Brains said.

He touched a button, the front of the plastic box opened out like a door. Behind it was a set of dials. There was a short thick rod fastened to the side of the box. Brains yanked it upward. It grew into a three-foot-high antenna, made of polished chrome.

"A radio transmitter," he explained. "I built it out of some surplus electronic parts. This transmitter broadcasts on the 11-meter citizens' band—the wavelength the government set aside for experimental purposes."

"But, Brains," I pleaded, "what's this all got to do with that man lurking out there?"

Brains hadn't even noticed my interruption. "On my way in here," he continued, "I stopped to install a battery-powered radio receiver in your tool shed."

He took a small microphone from his pocket and plugged it into the transmitter.

"When I speak into this microphone," Brains said, "that receiver will pick up the broadcast."

"So what," I said. "What good will that do?"

"Here's the plan," Brains said. "We'll talk into this mike and pretend to discuss the counterfeit coin. The prowler will hear the amplified conversation coming from the shed and slip closer to listen."

He looked up in triumph. "That's when we sneak up and *grab him!*"

"Never mind that we-stuff! Count me out," I said. "All I want to do is scare that guy into running."

"Operative Three, the spy out there may have important information on the Dexter case. At a time like this danger is unimportant. Benton and Carson expects every man to do his duty!"

It was no use protesting. Maybe I was the secretary-treasurer of Benton and Carson, but Brains was the *president*, and he was laying down the law.

"All right, X," I gulped. "We'll do it your way. What's the next step?"

"Into the living room and switch off the light," he snapped. "That will let our snooping friend know that you're leaving the living room. He won't know where to locate you—until he hears our voices coming from the tool-shed window."

Hey! This was beginning to sound like a crackerjack idea. I

slipped down the hall, doused the living room light, and returned to the kitchen.

Brains had carried the transmitter over to a chair near the window and was sneaking a look through the curtains.

"I can see him distinctly. He's crouching behind the privet hedges," Brains whispered. "He keeps watching the house, searching for you with those binoculars."

Brains pulled back from the window. "Now listen, Operative Three, when I switch on the microphone, we'll begin to ad lib about the coin. What you say doesn't have to make much sense, as long as it's about the counterfeit drachma."

I nodded. "All right, let's go. I'm with you."

It sounded crazy, but I'd seen Brains pull nuttier tricks than this that paid off.

He clicked on the mike switch and he gave me the high sign. We were on the air!

"Operative Three," Brains whispered loudly into the mike, "there are a number of unexplained circumstances in this case of the counterfeit drachma. I brought you out here so we could talk about them without being overheard."

He stopped and pointed to me. It was my turn.

"You're right, Chief," I said importantly. "We've got to get to the bottom of this unsavory business, no matter whom it hurts."

"Precisely my sentiments," answered Brains. "Now here's my plan for tomorrow. We'll start with the suspects in Bleeker City and . . ."

"Do you suggest another examination of the Curio Shop, Chief? Or were you thinking of the Coin and Stamp Exchange?"

Brains and I were peering through the curtain as we spoke over the mike. Outside in the fog I could see a hunched shadow scuttling toward the tool shed.

Brains' plan was working like a charm. The intruder had heard our voices echoing from the shed window, and he was taking the bait!

"Operative Three, what I am about to tell you now is top secret," Brains whispered hoarsely into the microphone.

Then, beckoning to me, he tiptoed toward the kitchen door. "Now here's the plan of action," he continued. He let his voice die down to a mumble. Then he gently lowered the microphone to a small work table close by and eased through the kitchen door. I was right behind him.

Outside I could see the prowler crouched beneath the shed window, waiting breathlessly for the details of tomorrow's plan. We had him hooked, but good!

Brains dug his elbow into my ribs. "Now!" he whispered.

We began to soft-shoe across the lawn. My heart was beating triple time. What with the fog and the way he was crouched over, it was hard to figure just how big this guy was. We had surprise on our side, but that didn't keep me from being scared stiff.

Suddenly, the prowler stood up. The abrupt silence in the shed was making him suspicious. He must have suspected a trap because he started to turn and look behind him.

That's when we grabbed him.

But it was like grabbing a buzz saw. This guy was small but he was all fists, knees and elbows. I got at least three good kicks in the shins, not to mention a clout on the ear with the binoculars.

Brains kept yelling orders to me.

"Hold him, Operative Three! Watch out for that leg!"

Then suddenly a sharp elbow rammed into his solar plexus.

Brains just leaned against the shed, his face kind of green and his glasses hanging from one ear. "Grab him," he wheezed.

The prowler had broken loose and was streaking across the wet lawn. He might have gotten away except for an old tree root that stuck out of the ground for a good three inches.

He hit the bad spot, tripped, and went zooming across the wet lawn on his face like a bobsled. He came skidding to a stop alongside the front walk.

Before he could get up I was straddling his back. Brains, still green from that belt in the stomach, was sitting on his feet. It was only then that I realized he was just a kid.

"Let me up! Let me up or I'll bash you!" The guy under us was bouncing like a Mexican jumping bean.

Brains and I looked at each other. That was the first time we had heard the kid's voice. We nearly flipped.

Our prowler was Terry Dexter!

# 11 DANGEROUS PROFESSION

Brother! Was that kid Terry ever sore!

She bounced up with her fists clenched.

"Okay," she gritted. "Put them up. I'll take both of you on together!"

Brains and I backed away.

Tackling some big tough goon was one thing. But we hadn't figured on running into this freckled-faced atom bomb.

I don't know what would have happened, but just then I heard somebody come up the sidewalk behind me.

"Terry Dexter!"

I turned. It was my sister Ann, back from the Dramatic Society.

"Oh, hello Ann," said Terry, flushing. She looked down and sort of shuffled her feet.

"Good gravy, Sis," I said. "Do you two know each other?"

"Of course we do. I was Terry's counsellor at camp." Ann turned to Terry, puzzled. "I haven't seen her since last summer. And here I find her fighting my brother right on our front lawn."

"This creep is your brother?" asked Terry pityingly. "Boy, I sure feel sorry for you with him for a relative. And that skinny redheaded stringbean isn't much better," Terry added, motioning to Brains.

"Now just a moment, all of you," said Ann, sounding just like my mother. "I saw that pitched battle on the lawn. Just what was it all about?"

Here it comes, I thought. Now Terry will spill the beans and tell Ann what happened in Bleeker City yesterday. And how we got her father in a jam. This was just going to be dilly.

But I didn't know Terry Dexter. This was a private fight and she didn't need anyone's help.

"I was just doing some bird watching," she said, and hiked her binoculars forward to show Ann. "And I thought I spotted a pair of long-nosed booby-hatches!"

She grinned as she spoke. I knew she was talking about Brains and me.

"We saw her snooping around here with those glasses," I told Ann. "Brains and I thought she was a prowler and nabbed her."

"Nabbed *me?* Ha!" snorted Terry. "It's a good thing your sister came along or I would have taken you two apart."

"For pity sakes," said Ann, "I can't make any sense of this squabbling! Into the house and clean up. All of you! Then we'll thrash this out."

When Ann talked like that you listened—or else! So Brains and I went in. Terry was right behind us. I guess Terry still thought a lot of Ann.

Brains and I used the upstairs bathroom to clean up. When we came down Ann had fixed three plates of ice cream on the kitchen table. Terry was already seated.

"All right, boys, sit down and grab your spoons. We're going to smoke the peace pipe," ordered Ann.

I couldn't see how you could smoke a peace pipe while eating ice cream, but I was willing to try. So was Brains.

"I haven't the time to hear this thing out," said Ann, heading for the front hallway. "I just dropped by to pick up a script for the Dramatic Society. They're all waiting for me. But I want you kids to promise me to settle this quarrel peacefully."

"Well," said Terry grudgingly. She didn't want to agree, but she was finding it hard to stay mad with a mouth full of ice cream.

"It's all right with me, Ann," I shrugged. "I didn't start this anyhow."

As for Brains, he put it in his own simple way. "We shall do our best to ameliorate our differences, Ann."

Whatever that meant.

Well, anyway, that's when Ann left us three alone.

But peace and quiet lasted only until Terry finished her ice cream. That was when she put down her spoon and said flatly, "One thing I'm telling you two. My father never saw those dies before you found them."

"But *somebody* put them there," I insisted. "They didn't just walk in by themselves."

"Now *there's* a shrewd observation," said Terry.

Brains thoughtfully inhaled a spoonful of ice cream. "Jimmy has made an important point, Terry. If your father didn't put them there, who did?"

"Look here," said Terry tautly, her eyes reddening. "My Dad's been in this business for twenty years. Nobody ever accused him of doing anything dishonest until you two buttinskies came along. Anyway, what makes you two so interested in that coin? If you ask me, you both know an awful lot about counterfeit coins for two innocent bystanders."

"So that's why you came sneaking around here with those binoculars," I said accusingly. "You were spying on us!"

Terry bristled. "I wanted to find out what's behind all this— and why you two snoops are hounding my father. What are you, a couple of private detectives?"

Brains cleared his throat importantly. "It may interest you to know, Terry, that we *are* private investigators."

Terry shot him a look. "Very amusing! If you two creeps are just going to make fun of me, I might as well . . ." She stood up to go. There were tears in her eyes.

"Terry, wait." Brains jumped up. "The firm of Benton and Carson would never dream of such discourtesy."

"*Benton and Carson?*" she gulped. "Who are they?"

Brains dug into his pocket and came up with a small white card.

"Here, have one of our business cards," he said importantly as he handed it to her.

I could have told her exactly what was printed on it. I memorized it word for word the day Brains printed them on the press he rigged up himself. It read:

## THE BENTON AND CARSON INTERNATIONAL DETECTIVE AGENCY
*Confidential Investigators and Criminologists*
*Modern Scientific Methods and Devices Used*

| SHADOWING | FREE CONSULTATIONS |
|---|---|
| TRACING OF MISSING PERSONS | 24-HOUR SERVICE |
| *President* | *Secretary-Treasurer* |
| Barclay "Brains" Benton | James "Jimmy" Carson |

"Jeepers!" said Terry, her eyes opening up as big as two soup plates. "You really *are* private detectives!"

Brains picked up the card. "You see, our firm was tracing the origin of that spurious drachma when we were involved in the unfortunate incident in your father's store."

Then Brains gave her the rundown on our investigation, from the time I found the drachma in my newspaper collection money right down to the minute the dies turned up in the Dexter store.

"Those dies!" said Terry when Brains finished. "You don't know how much trouble you caused when you found them."

"I'm sorry, Terry," said Brains, meekly. "We were only performing our duty."

Believe me, it sure was strange seeing Brains act so apologetically.

"I shouldn't cry, I know. But I'm so worried about my father."

That's when she told us her side of it. Terry's mother had died three years ago. After that her father developed a heart condition. That was why he took special pills.

The doctor had ordered him to avoid worries or shocks. But this counterfeiting business had really jolted him. Jeremy Dexter had worried himself into an attack.

"Do you realize what this is doing to him?" Terry asked hotly. "Nobody's going to buy anything in our shop after this."

She looked at us reproachfully. "I've been going crazy trying to figure out how those dies got there."

Brains frowned. "Terry, you need *professional* assistance," he said gravely. "The help of trained investigators using the latest scientific methods and devices."

"Skilled detectives who will track down every clue, trail every suspect." I piled it on.

"Hey, wait a minute." Terry brightened, suddenly, as our sales pitch hit her. "You two are private investigators! Couldn't you work for me?"

Brains leaned back and put the tips of his fingers together. "Then you wish us to represent you in this case?"

"Well, I don't know," said Terry, a little uncertain. "Are you *expensive?*"

Brains sort of tossed his hand as if the thought of money was unimportant to him.

"We won't discuss the question of a retainer for the present, but I think we can accept your father's case, Terry."

Boy! Did he sound like a big wheel!

Terry's eyes sparkled. "Gosh, that's wonderful! Wait till I tell Dad the news."

"I'm afraid that will be impossible." Brains frowned. "My partner and I work best as *undercover* agents. To reveal our identity to anyone would seriously hamper the investigation."

"Gosh, I wouldn't want to do that," she said in a small, guilty voice. "But I was wondering, how long will all this take?"

Brains pulled at his chin thoughtfully. "That is difficult to predict. We have several angles to investigate immediately."

"Ah, yes, there are some very intriguing questions that will bear investigation," I said, trying to sound like Brains.

Our client might as well know right now that I was a full-fledged partner in Benton and Carson.

Brains ignored the interruption and looked up at the ceiling. "First of all, there is the fact that Silas Gorme sold the drachma to Binky Barnes for twenty dollars. Five dollars less than he paid for it."

"Yes, but remember, Chief, he has an alibi for that," I reminded him. "He claims he was broke and had to do it."

Brains smiled faintly. "And yet one week later, when Gorme offered to pay Binky back his twenty dollars, he produced an unmistakably large roll of bills."

I'd clean forgotten that wad! Gorme's bankroll had been fat enough to strangle a horse!

"Heads-up thinking," I said admiringly.

"One more thing," Brains said. "When we first brought back the coin to Gorme, he took our word that the drachma was a fake. He never even bothered to examine it. He must have known from the first that it was counterfeit. Terry's father had to examine the drachma with great thoroughness before he pronounced it a fake."

You could see Brains hadn't missed a trick.

"But how can we explain away the dies that they found in the drawer?" Terry asked glumly. "That's the most important evidence against my father."

Brains began to pace the floor. "My associate and I have discussed that angle, Terry. We believe the dies were planted to point suspicion at your father."

"My father hasn't an enemy in the world," Terry said. "Who would do a terrible thing like that?"

"Who indeed?" muttered Brains. "When we have the answer to *that* question, the case will be solved."

He had that look he always gets when he's got his teeth in a case and is anxious to get started.

All of a sudden he turned and headed for the hallway. He stopped at the door of the kitchen.

"Operative Three," he said brusquely, "I must return to my laboratory. I am in the midst of some important experiments in infrared photography. We will proceed with the investigation tomorrow."

"Hey, wait!" yelped Terry. "How will I know what's going on?"

"All the clients of Benton and Carson receive regular daily progress reports, madam," Brains said. "Be assured that you will be kept fully informed at all times."

"But, can't I help?" she pleaded as we walked toward the front door. "I could be useful. I read lots of detective stories. Only last week I read a swell one called 'Kate Durward and the Emerald Eye.'"

Brains and I both shuddered.

"Please, Terry," I said. "Just leave the case in our hands. It takes the trained mind and sensitive eyes and ears of a skilled operative to match wits with criminals."

"Well, okay," said Terry reluctantly. "But any time you need a hand, just let me know."

She led the way outside and noisily hauled a battered bike from under our porch.

"Good grief, what a racket!" I said to Brains. "How in the world did she get that bike under the porch without me hearing her?"

"That's because you have the trained mind and sensitive eyes and ears of a skilled operative," said Brains with a lofty smile.

We waved good-by to Terry as she rolled down the street and vanished in the fog.

"Well, Brains, what's the schedule for tomorrow?" I queried.

"You will report to headquarters promptly at ten. After which we will proceed to investigate Silas Gorme and his Curio Shop. Get plenty of rest, you'll need it!"

And with that Brains, too, vanished into the mist.

I began shivering as I went back into the house. It wasn't the fog that chilled me.

I was thinking of Silas Gorme. And somehow just the idea of running into him again was enough to raise the goose flesh on my spine.

## 12 SPIES AT THE WINDOW

"Get plenty of rest," Brains had warned me. But that experience with Terry shadowing me in the fog had made me as jittery as a rabbit with an itch.

It took me hours to fall asleep. And when I finally did, I kept having one wild nightmare after another.

I kept getting lost in this big misty cave filled with all kinds of weird junk, like stuffed birds, wax dummies, shrunken heads and other gruesome stuff. Everywhere I went in that cave a huge vulture with a bald head, big beak and beady eyes kept swiping at me with his talons. And one of those talons was black!

But whenever I tried to escape the cave, Brains Benton would stop me.

"A trained operative knows no fear!" he would say. "You know your duty, Operative Three," and he'd shove me back into the cave.

I didn't need anyone to tell me what *that* dream meant. Silas Gorme really had me worried! The whole case was terrifying—and I was scared!

I woke up in the morning feeling like a candidate for the Happy Farm, but I doused my head with cold water and put on a bright smile when I came down to the kitchen.

After breakfast, I ran a couple of errands for my mother. Then, before I knew it, it was time to report to headquarters.

Brains was waiting for me at the curb outside his house when I arrived, and we headed our bikes toward the Turnpike.

"Aren't we taking an awful chance fooling around with this Gorme character?" I said. "If he's the kind who'd send a man to prison by planting those dies, he might be violent when cornered."

"A dangerous person indeed," Brains said. "But a private detective must learn to face peril courageously, Operative Three. Our duty is to investigate Silas Gorme—no matter what the risk!"

He sounded exactly the way he did when he was the star in my nightmare.

By then we were turning off at the Bleeker City exit of the Turnpike.

"All right," I said, "how do we handle it? Do we just barge in and question Gorme again?"

Brains looked at me as if I had suddenly developed two heads. "To interrogate Gorme now would put him on guard. We are going to make a reconnaissance."

We were near Gorcey Street, and the closer we got to the Curio Shop, the louder my nerves jangled.

"But how do we go about it?" I insisted. "We can't just hang around the front of the store and look through that dirty window!"

"Buildings are usually equipped with *rear* entrances, too," Brains said.

I could see he had an angle and was waiting until we came on the scene of operations before he tried it out, so I kept quiet.

We were a block from Gorme's place when Brains hopped off his bike. So did I. He nodded toward a narrow opening between two boarded-up buildings.

"We'll park our bikes in there, while we reconnoiter. We must make an unobserved approach!"

Brother, was that a laugh!

Because when we rolled up to that alley, a reception committee of one was waiting for us—a freckled-faced pony-tailed kid by the name of Terry Dexter!

"Hi, fellas," she said grinning. "I've been watching you coming up Gorcey Street. What are you doing here?"

"Who us?" I dead-panned. "We were making an unobserved approach to Gorme's store."

Brains grimaced. "How did you know we'd be here?" he snapped at Terry.

"Easy," was Terry's reply. "In the detective books I read they always investigate the hottest suspect first . . . that's Gorme. So I came down to see if I could help out."

That kid Terry was on the ball all right. But we needed her along like a hole in the head. This mission would be dangerous enough without a girl tagging along.

But that's where Brains surprised me. "As a matter of fact, Terry, you may be of use. Do you know anything about the streets and alleys in this neighborhood?"

"Do I? Just ask me," she said. "I used to live near here when we first moved into Bleeker City."

Brains stuck his head out of the alley and looked up the street toward the Curio Shop. Then he turned back to Terry. "Is there any way we can approach Gorme's store without being seen?"

Terry squinted, thinking hard. Then she brightened.

"Hey! I've got it! Just follow me!"

She darted out into the street, but headed *away* from Gorme's shop. Brains and I followed, wondering if she knew what she was doing.

She did. She led us clear around the entire square block and then ducked into a little alley that ran behind three clapboard houses right at the corner of Gorcey Street.

"This is the place!" whispered Terry.

Brains nodded. "Excellent," he said. "If my guess is correct, the center building is the one we want."

We slipped past the trash cans that crowded the mouth of the alley. Brains held a finger to his lips.

"From here on we will speak only in whispers," he hissed.

The buildings in that alley were a mess. Most of the windows were boarded up. Each of the three houses had a door on the alley and you got the idea that they weren't used for anything except to carry out trash.

We were partway down the alley when we noticed a wide space between Gorme's building and the last house in the row.

"That areaway may be just what we're looking for," Brains whispered.

Let me give you the picture. Out on Gorcey Street all three buildings were connected. But in the rear, the building with the Curio Shop was cut back for about five feet, leaving a space that allowed light to enter a side window on the first floor of Gorme's building.

That window proved the biggest break of all. When Brains spotted it, his face lit up like a Christmas tree.

Gesturing for silence, he crouched and tiptoed into the areaway. Terry and I watched him, not even daring to breathe.

Slowly, carefully, he raised his eyes above the sill to look inside. But this window was even dirtier than the display window out front. Brains shook his head in annoyance, then reached up and gently rubbed some of the dirt off the corner of the pane.

After that he raised his head again and peered in. He couldn't have been at that window for more than a few seconds, but to Terry and me it seemed like an hour.

When Brains ducked down again, I knew he'd seen something because he beckoned sharply to me.

My heart beating triple time, I crouched down and eased over to the window. Brains nodded upward. I knew he wanted me to look in.

Carefully, I put my eye against the clear spot on the window.

The glass was dirty on the inside, too, but I could still see a good deal. I was looking into the rear of the shop. It wasn't much different from the front—all cluttered with dusty knickknacks, stuffed animals and every kind of old junk you could dream of. Staring through that dirty window, everything looked kind of foggy inside.

I shuddered, remembering that crazy nightmare I'd had last night—the one about the foggy cave and the vulture.

And then, all of a sudden, I nearly fainted . . . because right there in front of me was the vulture himself—Silas Gorme!

He was working at a bench, his back to me. I could see he had something locked in a vise. I couldn't quite see what it was, but he kept tapping at it with a hammer and some small tool, like a chisel.

Once he turned and I saw he was wearing one of those eyepieces a jeweler uses when he's fixing a watch. Right then I could tell that he was working on something small and delicate.

Someone pulled at my sleeve. It was Terry.

"Jeepers," she hissed loudly. "You going to be up there all day? Give someone else a chance at that window."

I yanked my arm away. That kid had her nerve interfering with a detective on the job.

I looked through the window again—and nearly fell over. Gorme had stopped working, and for a minute I thought he had heard us. But he kept staring at something at the front of the shop. Then he took off his eyepiece—*and vanished!*

I ducked down.

"Brains," I whispered hoarsely. "He's gone, I can't see him anywhere."

Brains took a look. He kept turning his head every which way. I knew he was trying to spot Gorme. Then his face relaxed.

"I see him now," he said, his lips barely moving. "He's at the front door. There's a man—a postman I think—handing Gorme a package . . . wait! The postman has gone. . . . And here comes Silas!"

It was too much for me. I couldn't wait for Brains to tell me what was happening. I had to see it for myself. Before Brains could stop me, I reached up and wiped off another clear spot on the window.

Gorme was back in view again. He had a small package in his hand, and when he dropped it on the bench, it landed with a heavy thump that we could hear outside the closed window.

I put my mouth to Brains' ear.

"I wonder what's inside that package!" I said.

"We'll know in a moment, when he opens it," replied Brains.

But he didn't open it. Instead, Silas removed his apron and put on a jacket. Then he took the parcel and headed for the front of the shop.

Brains jumped up and so did I.

"He's leaving," Brains snapped.

"What do we do now?" said Terry frantically. "If he gets away we can't watch him!"

And then, without warning, she tore up the alley toward the street. "You wait here!" she called. "I'll see which way he's going."

"Terry, come back!" Brains said. But she was gone.

Brains put the palm of his right hand against his forehead and groaned. "Let us pray that Silas doesn't see her."

We knew she was coming back when a trash can cover clattered down the alley. I gulped, trying to keep my heart from popping out of my mouth.

Terry was almost in tears when she returned. "He left in a car. He was out of sight almost before I got to the corner. . . . Why didn't you guys follow me? We could have trailed him with our bikes."

"Calm yourself, madam," commented Brains. "Gorme's departure may be our golden opportunity."

Golden opportunity! What was he babbling about?

"But if Gorme's gone, who do we watch?" I asked.

Brains examined me scornfully. "We shall watch no one, but

proceed with the next step in our investigation—an on-the-spot survey of Gorme's shop."

He turned back to the window and began to push against the frame.

"You don't mean you're going to try to go in there?" I gasped. Trust Brains to cook up some risky stunt like this.

"Well, don't just stand there, Operative Three," he said impatiently. "Give me a hand with this window."

Terry looked worried. "You can't go in there! Suppose Silas comes back!"

"Yeah," I said. "Even if we do force the window and get inside—suppose we get caught? Silas could have us tossed in the clink and throw away the key! Or he might—well, if he's really a criminal—there's no telling *what* he might do."

"You seem a trifle pale, Operative Three," remarked Brains. "I recommend that your mother give you a tonic."

He simply ignored what I'd said. He reached up toward the top of the window frame again and began to push upward.

"Our course is clear, Operative Three. We're going to open this window and inspect the shop, no matter what the risk!"

"And that's where you're wrong, son," said a growling voice behind us.

We snapped around, all three of us. Standing at the mouth of the areaway, blocking all escape through the alley, was the dark, hulking figure of a man.

We were trapped!

# 13 SEARCH FOR A CLUE

We stood there motionless, the three of us.

I heard Brains suck in his breath. Terry sort of gasped.

Me? I was too paralyzed to do even that.

All I could do was to stare bug-eyed at the man blocking us from the alley. He was big, real big—like a brick wall—and you could see the muscles bulging under his blue suit. He had a dark, bristly mustache and a big cigar clamped in his teeth. He kept squinting at us through the smoke with a hard look.

And you got the idea that he could be pretty rough if he wanted to be.

"Now, just what were you kids trying to do?" he growled. His voice was deep and it kind of boomed from the walls of the areaway. It seemed to come from all around us.

I didn't know what to say. Right then I was so scared that my mind went completely blank.

But not Brains. He'd been just as frightened as I, but he bounced back fast!

"I know this looks suspicious, sir," he said smoothly. "But you see we happened to wander into this alley and we were wondering where this window leads."

"It could lead to a lot of trouble, son," rumbled the big man, frowning. "Who are you kids, anyhow? Talk up, and *fast!*"

Brains was about to speak when suddenly the big man yanked out his cigar and pointed it at Terry.

"Say! I know you. You're the Dexter kid! Jeremy Dexter's girl, aren't you?"

"Y-yes," admitted Terry. Her voice was trembly. Terry Dexter was usually plenty spunky but right then she wasn't.

"Know who *I* am?" asked the big man, shoving the cigar back into his teeth. He shot the question at her like a detective.

"I-I think so. You're Mr. Devlin, from the real estate company."

"That's it, sister," the man called Devlin replied. "I happen to own the three buildings on this alley. I was in the neighborhood when I saw you charge out and watch Mr. Gorme drive away."

Brains and I exchanged looks. It was just what we had been afraid of when Terry had raced after old Gorme. The fat was in the fire.

"Let's get back to the main question," grunted Devlin. He speared Brains and me with a sharp look. "What were you kids doing back here at that window? You'd better do the talking, Terry. I don't know these other two."

Terry looked at Brains and then at me, as if asking us what to do. Brains nodded the go-ahead. And I just prayed that she wouldn't try inventing some screwball story. This guy Devlin was no fool. He'd spot a phony yarn a mile away.

But Terry took a deep breath and right there, standing in the alley, she told him the only thing she could—the truth. All about the counterfeit coin and Silas Gorme. And how the dies were found in her father's store. And how her Dad was slated to go before the Grand Jury as a counterfeiter.

Once Brains and I got a scare when we thought she was going

to blurt out the fact that she'd hired us as private investigators, but Terry had enough sense to catch herself before she'd done any damage. The firm of Benton and Carson was never mentioned.

All the time Devlin was listening to her he kept puffing on that cigar and sort of squinting at us. He had a deadpan expression on his face, so we couldn't tell whether he believed Terry or not. But as the story went on, he kept puffing faster and faster, as if he were working up a head of steam.

When Terry finally finished, Devlin yanked the cigar out of his mouth. His face was red and mad-looking.

"Terry," he grated, "I've just come back from an out-of-town trip so this is all news to me. . . . But I'll say this. Jeremy Dexter is an honest man. And anyone who'd accuse him of being a counterfeiter is crazy."

When I realized Devlin believed our story, I let go with a gasp of relief.

But Devlin wasn't done with us, yet.

"You kids haven't been very smart," he commented. "You can't go around playing detective on your own. That sort of thing could get you into a mess of trouble."

*Playing* detective! Boy, wouldn't Devlin keel over if he found out that Brains and I were the real McCoy.

"Tell you what I can do," Devlin was saying. He tipped his hat back and blew a big ring of smoke. "As the president of the Devlin Real Estate Company I have a duplicate set of keys to Gorme's store. There's a back door here. Suppose I open it and let you have a look inside for yourselves."

Talk about a lucky break! Brains and I nearly took off like a couple of Fourth of July rockets!

As he stepped from the areaway and let us out into the alley, Devlin took a bunch of keys from his pocket. He picked out one of them and slipped it in the lock of the back door.

"To tell the truth, I don't know much about this Silas Gorme, even though he's been a tenant of mine for a couple of years," said Devlin. "If he's mixed up in some shady business, I want to know about it."

The lock clicked and Devlin pushed the door open. "Wait out here," he said. "I'll go in first and have a look!"

Brains looked after him disapprovingly.

"For Pete's sake, don't complain," I whispered. "You ought to be tickled pink this guy Devlin is on our side."

We could hear Devlin rummaging around, opening and closing drawers and apparently examining things. And the more racket he made the more annoyed Brains became.

"What's he *doing* in there?" Brains said irritably. "For all we know he may be accidentally destroying clues. Or he could be disturbing things enough for Gorme to notice and put him on his guard."

A minute later Devlin came to the door, his face dead serious as he clamped down on his cigar. "You're right, kids, Gorme was working on something at that bench."

Then all of a sudden Devlin's face broke up into a big grin.

I didn't get it. If we caught Gorme working on something crooked, what was so funny?

"Suppose you all come in and see what Gorme was working on," said Devlin, chuckling.

"Thank you, sir," said Brains, "I should appreciate the opportunity to investigate the premises personally."

We pushed our way into the back of the shop past barrels filled with old crockery and bundles of moldy magazines. There were cobwebs and dust everywhere. The place made you think of bats and black widow spiders.

Believe me, I sure was glad there was a grownup like Devlin in there with us.

Devlin pushed past us and switched on a light over Gorme's bench. "Here, kids, take a look for yourselves!"

The bench was covered with a scattering of tools, hammers, chisels and files. And right in the middle of the whole shebang was a big, old-fashioned cuckoo clock!

Brains gulped audibly. This was the end. After all the shrewd deductions, guesswork and suspicions, the whole case was blowing up in our faces.

But Brains wasn't giving up yet. "I should like to examine that clock, if I may, Mr. Devlin."

"Of course, son, go right ahead," was the reply.

Brains stepped up to the bench and lifted the clock. There was a gritty sound beneath his feet and he looked down.

"Some metal chips down there," Devlin said. "Stepped on them myself. I meant to warn you."

"Quite all right, sir," Brains said.

He examined the clock briefly and then put it down.

"Mr. Devlin, now that we're inside, do you mind if I have a look around?" Brains asked, innocently.

Devlin frowned. "Well, all right," he said with some reluctance. "But I didn't find anything. Don't take too long."

"I will make my examination as brief as possible," Brains said.

He began to prowl around the shop, poking into cartons, barrels and boxes. I didn't know what he was after, but he had that bird-dog look again.

Devlin followed Brains with his eyes. He had a funny kind of smile as he watched and then he turned to me.

"Is your friend always like that?" he asked in a loud whisper. I knew Brains had heard it.

As if that wasn't enough, Devlin reached over to the cuckoo clock and tripped a little lever. A door flew open near the top of the clock and the little carved bird inside shot out and spoke his piece.

"Cuckoo! Cuckoo!" it said, about half a dozen times.

I saw Brains flush red. But to Devlin this was just one big howl. He laughed loudly, and even Terry giggled a little.

Some people have a strange sense of humor and I guess this Devlin was one of them.

But the gag got under my skin. Brains was my partner and no one was going to pull anything like that on him.

"You don't have to worry about Brains, sir. He knows exactly what he's doing," I said hotly.

Maybe it did look funny to someone who didn't know Brains —seeing him snooping around like that. But I knew that his eyes were registering, measuring and recording everything that he saw. Weeks from now he'd be able to remember every detail of that shop with the accuracy of a sharp photograph.

Anyhow, after another couple of minutes Brains was finished. If he had found any worthwhile clue, he didn't say anything.

"Thank you for your cooperation, sir," he said to Devlin. "I'm through with my examination."

"Glad to help, son," said Devlin. "But now I think we ought to get out of here. That old bird Gorme may be coming back soon. I wouldn't want him to find us here. I'd have a tough time explaining why I let you in."

Devlin let us out into the alley and locked the door.

Out on the street he spoke to Terry. "I'm sorry about your dad," he said. "Tell him not to worry. I'll have a talk with Gorme. He's my tenant, you know. Perhaps I can talk him out of pressing the charges."

This Devlin sounded like a swell guy after all.

"Thanks, Mr. Devlin," said Terry. "Thanks a lot."

"That's all right," he answered.

There was a nifty red sedan at the curb. He started to get in it, then beckoned to me and Brains.

"Look, boys," he said in a sort of father-son way, "snooping around like that can be a very dangerous game. If anyone else had caught you in that alley, you'd have been in a king-size jam. So, if you run into any more information on this case, just bring it to me. I'll be glad to help out any way I can."

You can see that Mr. Devlin was on our side—all the way.

After he drove away, Brains and I walked Terry to the alley where we had parked our bikes. Now that the search was over we all felt the letdown.

Especially Terry. She was really in the dumps.

"I was hoping we'd find some real evidence in Gorme's place —evidence to clear my father. But it looks like we hit a dead end."

She bit her lip, trying hard not to cry. "We've got to do *something*. Dad heard from Judge Parker. His Grand Jury hearing is set for next week, and he's worried sick."

Brains tried to perk her up. "Terry, we've only just started our investigation. We have half a dozen angles to explore."

She tried to force a smile. But she couldn't say anything. She just sort of waved as she rode off.

We headed for Crestwood, Brains pedaling silently all the way. I could see his think-tank was churning hard and he didn't want me to bother him with questions.

So I left him alone till we braked to a stop in front of my house. Then, I said, "Well, all right, what's the next step?"

Brains shook his head. "Frankly, Jimmy, I don't know."

This didn't sound one bit like Brains.

"Wait a minute," I said, sharply. "You told Terry we had half a dozen angles to explore."

"I guess you could call that a white lie," said Brains. "It's bad for our reputation when a Benton and Carson client is that discouraged."

He kicked at the curb. "The whole morning has been a flop. I was so sure we'd find proof of counterfeiting activity in Gorme's shop, but it proved to be just a blind trail." He ran his fingers through his hair. "I'm plain stumped, Jimmy. Stumped!"

That floored me. What I mean is that Brains was always so smart and on the ball! During an investigation he always had some new angle or other that would keep us moving on the case.

But not this time.

"Well, there is no point in wasting time standing here," said Brains in disgust. "I believe I'll go up to the laboratory. I must continue my experiments in infra-red photography."

I tried to cheer myself up. Brains' working on an experiment was always a good sign.

Maybe you've read how Sherlock Holmes always played the violin for inspiration whenever a case had him up a tree. Well, it was just like that with my partner. Only Brains used his experiments to calm himself down and help him think his way out of a hole.

Yeah, I was pretty certain that sooner or later old X would pull a rabbit out of a hat and we'd get started on the case again.

And brother, was I right!

I planned to drop in on Brains at headquarters right after supper, about eight o'clock. But it didn't work out.

It was one of those days when everything goes haywire. First of all the County waited until 3:00 P.M. to release the news of a big highway plan. Of course, the *Ledger* had to break up the front page and delay the presses for an *extra*. That meant I couldn't start on my route until an hour later.

And as if that wasn't enough, I got a blowout in my back tire on Tinker Drive, and I had to traipse all over creation, pushing my bike by hand. After that I had to walk across town to leave the bike at the repair shop.

Of course I was late for supper. Everyone was all finished by the time I came home, so I had to eat by myself.

I was almost done when my mother said, oh so casually, "By the way, Barclay called. He wants you to call him right away."

"Right away!" I nearly choked on a chunk of pie. "How long ago was this?"

"Oh, about five o'clock, I'd say."

Yipes! And here it was after eight by the kitchen clock!

I choked down the last of my pie, ducked into the hallway and grabbed the phone.

Brains was waiting for my call. "Operative Three, you are to report to headquarters at once. *Satellite Zeta is in orbit!*"

Without another word he hung up.

The case must have broken wide open. Why else would he send that secret code message? I had to get over to the lab, and I had to get there *fast!*

# 14 SUSPICION

But I had to pull out all the stops to get permission from Dad to leave the house.

"It's past eight-thirty," he pointed out. "It wouldn't hurt if you occasionally spent an evening at home, son."

"Well, for Pete's sake. This is important, Dad," I said. "I've got a *problem* to work out with Brains."

You should have seen my father's face light up. "A problem, hey? I'm glad to see you finally getting serious about your math. And that Benton boy is just the one to help you with your algebra. All right, son. You can go."

I went.

After all, it wasn't my fault Dad thought it was a *math* problem that had me so excited.

It was close to nine when I reached headquarters. As I came up through the secret passageway, Brains was hobbling up and down with a curious limp.

"X, what's *wrong?* Are you hurt?" I said anxiously.

I stared down at his feet. He was clumping around the room

wearing one sneaker. All he wore on the other foot was a sock.

"Stop being ridiculous," he snapped. "Please step this way. I have something vital to show you."

I followed him to a table. He had the magnifier set up. It was the same gadget he had used to examine the fake drachma. Next to the magnifier lay the other sneaker. I was tempted to ask what it was doing there but something told me to clam up and wait for further developments.

Brains snapped on the light in the magnifier.

"Be good enough to examine the specimen I have mounted under the lens," he commanded.

I looked into the eyepiece. There, under the bright light of the bulb, I saw a cluster of small particles. They were sharp-edged and glittering.

"They look like small chips and grains of metal to me," I said.

"Precisely," he replied, with his best mastermind frown. "They are of the finest steel."

He gestured toward a group of test tubes lined up in a holder on a nearby table.

"My analysis shows these chips come from the grade of steel that is used for dies—the kind of die that minted the counterfeit drachma."

I blinked. This was leading up to something. But what?

"All right, I'll bite," I said. "Where did you get these chips?"

"From that pile of grit near Gorme's workbench," he informed me. "When I stepped on the pile of grit some of it became imbedded in the rubber sole of my sneaker."

He chuckled. "It would have escaped my attention completely except for Mrs. Ray."

"Mrs. Ray? For Pete's sake, how would she know about some chips of steel stuck in your sneakers?" I asked.

"She complained that I had marred the wax job she had just finished on our kitchen floor."

"Brains, do you know what this means?" I yelled as the truth hit me.

Brother! What a silly question. Brains was way ahead of me.

"It seems to indicate that Silas Gorme was almost certainly working on dies at his bench," Brains said. "And most likely some kind of counterfeit dies. Those chips and filings are a dead giveaway."

"He probably hides the dies somewhere whenever he goes out," I guessed. "That cuckoo clock was just a cover-up."

Now that we were off and running again, I was anxious to get started. "Well, Brains, what's the next step now? How do we proceed?"

"Now that we feel sure that Silas was working on counterfeit dies, we know that the evidence is most certainly in his shop. We just have to search the premises more thoroughly."

I snapped my fingers. "Hey! That Mr. Devlin, Gorme's landlord! He offered to help out whenever we needed him. As a matter of fact, he told us to be sure to notify him if there were any new developments."

"Mr. Devlin! Of course," nodded Brains, as he began to pull on his sneaker. "This evidence should convince him to let us make a really thorough search of the Curio Shop."

He finished tying his sneaker and straightened up. "Very well then, we can say good night now, Operative Three," he said. "We have had a most grueling day. Let us hope that tomorrow will be more rewarding. . . . Please report here promptly at nine. I shall want you to accompany me when I visit Mr. Devlin."

"Holy smoke!" I blurted. "I just remembered something! We never asked him his address. We don't even know where to look for him."

Brains gave me a pitying stare. "The telephone directory could be helpful," he said.

I winced.

As he ushered me out of the lab, he shook his head sadly. "Operative Three, I sometimes wonder if you were cut out to be a private investigator."

I should have resented that remark, but I was so tickled about the new lead that it went almost completely over my head.

I headed home wondering how I was ever going to wait until the next morning.

But getting to Brains' house on time the next day wasn't that easy. The complications set in at breakfast.

Since I had that week off from school, Dad left orders that I wasn't to leave the house till I cut the lawn.

I rushed through breakfast, hauled the lawn mower out of the shed and began to cut the grass. But believe me, I didn't have my heart in it. No matter how often I trimmed that grass it always needed a cutting before the week was out.

What beats me is my father spending all that money for fertilizer just to make the grass grow—and me spending half my youth cutting it down. I was beginning to wonder if I shouldn't have a serious talk with Dad about paving the lawn with concrete.

Well, I finally finished the job. But just as I was starting to get my bike I suddenly remembered it was still at the bike shop being fitted with a new tire.

I could see it was going to be one of those days again.

I headed for Brains' house, running all the way. I didn't want him leaving for Bleeker City without me.

He was waiting at headquarters and looking at his watch as I reported in. That was when I told him about my bike. I figured he'd be sore. But he just shrugged and remarked that he'd give me a lift to the bike shop on his handle bars.

It was all the way across town, with a couple of stiff grades in between. When we reached there, Brains' face was red and he was puffing like a steam engine.

Bailing out the bike cost me a small fortune. But money was the last thing on my mind as we shot down the Turnpike toward Bleeker City.

Benton and Carson, that pair of human bloodhounds, were on the trail!

As we came off the Turnpike at Bleeker City, Brains said, "I looked Devlin up in the phone book. His office is at 528 Broadway."

"Swell," I said. "This exit leads right onto Broadway. All we have to do is go straight ahead."

Brains shook his head. "A roundabout course might be more advisable, Operative Three."

I gave him an inquiring frown. I didn't get this.

"Terry," he reminded me curtly.

I got it. "I read you loud and clear, Chief," I announced.

We cut down a side street and then turned right on another thoroughfare that ran parallel to Broadway. That way we would avoid passing the Dexter store and maybe getting all tangled up with our client.

After a few blocks we turned down a tree-lined street and cut over to Broadway.

You probably think dodging around like that just to avoid a little snip of a girl was crazy.

And maybe it was. But that was the luckiest thing we ever did. Just wait until I tell you why.

We were about to turn into Broadway when suddenly Brains grabbed me by the arm!

I jammed on my brakes so hard I darn near went zooming over the handle bars.

"What is it?" I said hoarsely.

He never answered. He just hopped off his bike and shoved it against the brick wall of the corner building.

I didn't know what this was all about, but I was right behind him.

An instant later he was hugging the building and poking his head around the corner to sneak a look at something.

He'd probably seen Terry and didn't want her to see us, I thought.

Just then Brains beckoned frantically to me. I slipped up along the wall and crouched down right in front of him. Then

I stuck my head out beyond the building line and sneaked a look. I nearly fell over.

It was *Silas Gorme!*

He was walking down along the opposite side of Broadway, pretending to look into the windows. But he wasn't window shopping by a long shot. He kept glancing back over his shoulders as if he was afraid of being followed. If ever I saw a man act suspiciously, it was Silas Gorme.

He was toward the corner when he came to a narrow doorway alongside a store front. Once again he shot a worried glance up and down Broadway and then he opened the door, ducked inside and vanished.

Brains plucked at my sleeve. We pulled back.

"Did you see that?" I asked. "The way he kept looking back over his shoulder! Brother, he was scared stiff that somebody would see where he was going."

"Yes," said Brains. "And did you observe by any chance *where* he was going?"

"No, I didn't," I said. "I don't get it. What're you driving at?"

"Take another look, Operative Three," Brains said, nudging me toward the corner. "And this time *use your eyes!*"

I did. And what I saw really staggered me. Gorme had entered the doorway of number 528 Broadway—the *address of the Devlin Real Estate Company*.

I could see the lettering of the company name on two of the three windows of the second floor. There was a third window directly over the doorway. But the only sign there read: FOR RENT.

I turned back to Brains. "What's he doing up in Devlin's office? Maybe he's just paying his rent," I guessed.

Brains pursed his lips. "I doubt it. This is the twenty-fifth of the month. It's too early to pay rent for May and much too late to pay for April."

"Well, maybe Devlin is seeing Gorme to put in a good word for Mr. Dexter. Remember, he promised to do that."

"Perhaps," Brains muttered. "And yet, why did Gorme keep looking back over his shoulder? It just doesn't add up."

Brains sneaked another look around the corner and so did I.

"Jimmy," he said, "do you see what I see?"

Did I! Up on the second floor Harry Devlin was pulling down the window shade. Right down to the bottom!

"Strange that he should draw the blinds," said Brains. "There's no sunshine on that side of the street. It would seem that Devlin might have something to hide. He obviously doesn't want anyone to spot Gorme in his office."

"Brains," I said. "There's a big, fat skunk in the woodpile. I'm beginning to get the smell."

# 15  DOUBLE CROSS

"What do we do now?" I asked, anxiously.

"It is quite clear that we must try to discover what those two are so anxious to hide. I'm afraid we'll have to do some eaves-dropping, Operative Three."

I looked at him, stupefied. "You mean we're going to slip into that building and listen in? Suppose they see us?"

"Most unlikely," Brains replied. "The blinds are drawn. If we can't see Gorme and Devlin, they most likely can't see us."

He stepped out onto Broadway. "Just stroll casually across the street and into the building."

*Stroll,* he said. It was all I could do to walk.

Somehow I made it across the street. Then we were walking down the block toward number 528. When we came to the entrance, he eased the knob around and slipped through the door without a sound.

Me? I was standing there too scared to make a move—until Brains grabbed me by the arm and yanked me inside.

"Don't just stand there," he hissed. "You'll attract attention."

Gently he closed the door behind us. We were at the foot of a narrow stairway that led to the landing on the second floor. The steps were thickly carpeted and on the upper landing we could see a neatly painted sign reading:

DEVLIN

REAL ESTATE COMPANY

*OFFICE*

By hugging the left-hand wall of the vestibule and stretching our necks we could make out the frosted window glass on the entrance to Devlin's office.

From behind the door came the boom of an angry voice. It was Devlin. And with every other word there was a heavy thumping sound. You got the idea he was ripping mad and pounding his desk to prove it.

Gorme was there, too. Now and then you could hear him trying to interrupt in a whining voice. But Devlin wasn't listening. You could tell he was laying down the law and that he had Gorme jumping through the hoop.

But we couldn't make out exactly what they were saying. The way that hallway was made all you could hear was a lot of rumbling echoes.

"Brains," I whispered. "This is dangerous. We can't stay here."

"You're right, Operative Three. We're going upstairs."

He pulled at my arm.

"Upstairs? If Devlin and Gorme hear us . . ."

"Not a chance, Jimmy, not with all that hullaballoo going on!"

He started catfooting up the stairway.

Every bit of common sense I had, told me to stay where I was. Or better yet, to get out of that building. But *fast!*

Yet who was it that followed X up the stairs? How right you are. It was old faithful, foolish, Operative Three!

Sure, I was scared. I was so scared that I couldn't understand why my feet were following Brains upstairs when I wanted them to go the other way.

It was only about twenty steps to the second-floor landing but to me it seemed like climbing Mt. Everest. By the time I got to the top, I didn't know whether the oxygen was giving out or whether I was just too scared to breathe.

Brains reached the top before me. I saw him crouched outside the door of Devlin's office, listening.

Beyond him I could see the door to another office down at the front end of the hall. There had been some lettering on the frosted glass, but now it was partly scraped off. I figured it must be the empty office that was for rent.

I tiptoed over to Brains' side, and tuned in on the conversation between Devlin and Gorme. Their voices were a lot clearer up here. They were still a little rumbly with echoes, but I could make out what they were saying.

Devlin was yelling like mad. "Gorme, you're an utter fool! I warned you and warned you about peddling those counterfeits on your own. You risked the entire setup just for a few lousy bucks."

"Take it easy, Devlin," Gorme said. It was a cinch to identify his high-pitched voice. "I didn't mean any harm."

But Devlin apparently wasn't to be hushed. His voice boomed out even louder and angrier.

"You could have landed us all in the pen. And maybe you will yet."

"Now look, Boss," Gorme said. You could just tell he was cringing under the tongue lashing. "You've got to admit that I did my best to get back that drachma I sold to the Barnes kid. And I would've except for a bad break. How was I to tell that

that newspaper kid Carson would get the coin by mistake? Even then only foul luck kept me from grabbing it in the drugstore."

I stared wide-eyed at Brains. Good gravy! It looked as if Gorme hadn't been in Saffron's Drugstore entirely by accident, after all. I could see that Brains was soaking up the conversation so eagerly his ears were almost stretching.

"You make me sick, Gorme!" Devlin said. "You bungle everything you touch. Why did you have to get mixed up with this man Dexter?"

"Well, maybe I did slip up there. I just bought the original drachma from him so that I could make up a master copy. But don't worry about trouble. When things got hot, I planted my dies in Dexter's shop—and tricked that smart-aleck kid Benton into finding them. Now the finger is pointing right at Jeremy Dexter, and I'm in the clear."

Brains looked mad enough to bite nails at how he'd been used to do Gorme's dirty work. And me? Well, Jimmy Carson, Operative Number Three, had become *sucker number one!*

"You're *not* in the clear!" came Devlin's snarling voice. "Those kids Benton and Carson smell a rat. I caught them hanging around the back of your store yesterday, with that Dexter girl tagging along. I let them into your shop, and . . ."

"Let them into . . ." Gorme said. "Are you crazy?"

"Crazy like a fox. I went in first to clear away any possible evidence. They think you were working on a cuckoo clock. They don't suspect a thing."

I winced. Devlin had really pulled the wool over our eyes.

"I pulled the big-brother act on them," Devlin said. The anger in his voice had been replaced by a note of boasting. "I fed them the old soft soap and promised to get you to drop the charges against Dexter. They think I'm helping them. They've even promised to come to me with any new information."

There was the sound of laughter and Brains and I turned red. Boy, had we been taken.

"Devlin, you sure are a smart one," Gorme said. "With you

in charge, everything will be O.K. I'll try not to make any more mistakes."

Gorme had put so much of the old oil into his words, you could almost smell it. But it must have worked on Devlin. For when he spoke again, he sounded friendly.

"Well, all right, all right," he said. "Now, tell me. How's the big job coming?"

"Fine," replied Gorme. "The die work is nearly complete. It's going to be a dilly!"

"Good! We can begin minting that big one the minute you finish. I managed to round up a good stock of supplies while I was away. They're being shipped in right now," said Devlin.

"I know," grunted Gorme. "I got a package yesterday. I brought them right over to the plant."

"Good," said Devlin, approvingly. "Now you'd better get back to the shop and get cracking on those dies."

Brains looked at me and motioned toward the stairway.

He didn't have to warn me. Gorme would be coming through the office door in a couple of seconds. This was our cue to clear out.

We were at the head of the stairs when, without warning, we heard the rattle of the knob on the downstairs door.

Behind us, in the office, Gorme and Devlin had heard the sound too.

"Someone's coming," hissed Devlin. "Could be one of the boys."

Right then the downstair's door began to swing open.

That stairway was the only way in or out of the building!

We were caught in the middle, *with no place to hide*.

# 16 SECRET OPERATIONS

Brother, were we in a jam! I shot Brains a look that said, "What do we do now?"

He gestured frantically, pointing behind me.

*The vacant office in the front hall!* It was our only chance.

And with the newcomer thumping up the stairway we'd better grab that chance fast!

We tiptoed back along the deep carpet of the hall praying that the empty office wouldn't be locked.

Talk about luck! The door opened at a touch. We slipped inside and closed it behind us.

For the moment we were safe. We'd made it by a split second. But I'd be twitching for a week.

Outside in the hallway I could hear the newcomer coming up to the landing. Just then I noticed Brains was leaning up against the frosted glass of the door. He'd be spotted for sure!

With a lightning move, I yanked Brains aside. Then I pointed at the glass. I didn't have to draw him a picture. He knew it had been a close call.

Brains nodded his thanks. I felt like I'd won a battle citation.

Suddenly Devlin's voice boomed in the hall. He must have opened his office door to admit the visitor.

"Oh, Whisper! Come on in! There's nobody here but Gorme and me. What's up? Anything wrong at the plant?"

The door must have closed. I couldn't make out if the man called Whisper answered or not. There were too many rumbling echoes down at our end of the hall.

But all of a sudden they were all out in the hall again walking to the stairs. I could hear Devlin say, "Okay, Whisper, I'll come out to the plant and see if I can straighten things out."

I heard him lock his office door.

"Gorme," Devlin added, "we'll be ready to roll that new Roman Stater tonight. I want you to inspect the first run."

Gorme mumbled an answer that sounded like, "Okay."

"Let's get going," snapped Devlin. "Gorme, you first. And make sure no one spots you."

Gorme went. We heard him leaving through the street door. Then the other two followed him.

Brains pulled me toward the window. We sneaked a look. Silas was across the street, hurrying down Broadway toward Gorcey Street.

Devlin and the one they called Whisper came into view below us. Whisper was a smallish man, thin-shouldered and very pale. He seemed to walk with no effort at all. Just sort of float along. I got the idea he could be a bad guy to tangle with. Then they climbed into Devlin's red sedan and drove away.

"It's over," said Brains. "You may now resume breathing."

That may sound like a joke. But believe me, it wasn't.

"Let's get out of here, *fast!*" I said.

Brains never answered. He sprinted down the stairway two steps at a time and I was right behind him. A minute later we were on our bikes, streaking for Crestwood.

And we didn't stop until we were back at headquarters.

Up in the lab Brains pulled open the drawer of a filing cabinet and extracted a well-filled folder.

"What's that?" I said. He let me have a closer look. Lettered on the folder I read:

JEREMY DEXTER CASE

"Since we now have a client, I thought it wise to begin an accurate file of all our cases," said Brains. "Some day private investigators of the future will consult our records to learn the most advanced techniques of criminology!"

Wouldn't that floor you? The ideas in that carrot-topped head of his!

He took the file to his desk, opened it and began to write.

"Excuse me, Operative Three, I wish to record the conversation we heard in Devlin's office before I forget all the important details."

It took him a few minutes to put it all down. I waited until he was finished.

"Look, Brains," I said, "do you really think Gorme came to Doc Saffron's drugstore to try to get the coin from me? If so, how did he know I had it?"

Brains leaned back in his chair. "I've been going over that episode in my mind ever since we listened to their interesting conversation. The coincidence of Gorme being in the drugstore at the time you discovered you had Binky's drachma had worried me from the very start. It was just too fortuitous to be credible."

"Then, how do you explain it?" I asked.

Brains was silent for a moment. "All we can do, at present, is make a supposition," he said. "Proof will have to come later. However, I believe that Devlin, enraged that Gorme was selling counterfeits on his own, demanded that Gorme get back as many of the coins as he could. This, Gorme tried to do. I am of the opinion that Gorme came into Saffron's Drugstore preparatory to making a survey of the Barnes' house. Remember it is very close by. Gorme was in the act of making a telephone call when you stepped into the next booth. He, of course, overheard your conversation about the coin and . . ."

Brains spread his hands. "That is how it probably occurred."

I nodded. Yeah, it made sense the way Brains put it.

"But right now, Operative Three," Brains said, "we have graver matters to concern us. This case has become much bigger than we ever dreamed."

"Boy, you're not kidding," I said. "At first we thought we were only up against Gorme. Now, there's that two-faced, double-crossing guy Devlin. And the one they called Whisper. And who knows how many more Devlin has in his gang!"

"The problem is what do we do now?"

"I'll tell you what we do," I announced. "We're going right down to the police, that's what."

"Out of the question," Brains said curtly. "Thus far we have nothing to back our story except a few chips of steel and some hearsay conversation. The authorities would never believe us. All we would do is put Devlin and his men on guard."

"All right, then, what's next?" I challenged. "You tell me!"

"We could try to locate that plant we heard them talking about," said Brains.

I shuddered violently at the thought. Oh, no! Please, not *that!*

"It could be right here in Bleeker City or twenty miles away," Brains continued. "It might take days to locate the spot, and we are fighting for time."

"Fighting for time?" I asked. I didn't get it!

"This is Tuesday. Our Easter vacation will be over next Monday. That gives us just five days to solve the case before school begins."

"That's right," I agreed with him. "School would complicate things. We'll have to work fast!"

"Precisely," said Brains. "And I believe we will get the quickest results by investigating the Curio Shop once more."

"You're crazy! Absolutely out of your mind!"

Then I nearly blew my stack. "After yesterday, Gorme and Devlin will be on their guard. It'll be like poking your head into a very active hornet's nest!"

"Nonsense," Brains said confidently. "They won't expect us to return—especially now that Mr. Devlin has so cleverly pulled the wool over our eyes with his big-brother act!"

There was just a hint of a smile on Brains' lips. I could see that this Devlin character was in for a rough time before this was all over.

But I was far from convinced that the plan would work.

"We'll probably have to watch the place for days before we have a chance to get in there."

"Not at all," Brains reminded me. "Gorme is apparently meeting with Devlin somewhere tonight. We may, therefore, be in luck and find the Curio Shop unguarded."

He stood up and closed the case folder. "Please report at seven-thirty tonight, ready for duty, Operative Three!"

As far as Brains was concerned the discussion was *over*.

But *I* wasn't finished by a long shot. I told Brains a battalion of marines couldn't drag me within a mile of Gorcey Street again. I told him it was probably illegal to force our way into the shop even though we knew we were dealing with counterfeiters, and that if any of the gang spotted us we'd be sure to get hurt.

It could even mean our finish!

Brains listened to all my arguments. But I might as well have saved my breath.

For that night at eight when Brains Benton was slipping into the alley behind the Curio Shop, I was with him.

Believe me, going into that alley after dark was like stepping into the tunnel of horror. There was a street lamp near the corner, but only a little light reached the alley, just enough to show the trash cans at the entrance.

Once we parked our bikes and pushed past the cans we were in total darkness.

"Flashlight," whispered Brains, reaching back with his hand like a surgeon for a scalpel.

I slipped the flashlight to him and he switched it on. The result was a faint yellow beam. Brains grunted in disgust.

"For pity sakes," he muttered, "you could have at least tested the battery before you brought it along."

I didn't have the time to feel foolish. I was too busy groping in the darkness, trying to keep up with Brains.

I still get the cold creeps when I remember that night in the alley. Especially when the flash picked out two green glowing eyes just before something scrambled between my legs and scuttled over a fence.

I nearly jumped out of my skin, then and there! I would have taken off like a guided missile if Brains hadn't been there to grab my arm.

"Idiot!" he snapped, "it was only a cat!"

I was an idiot all right—for letting him talk me into this nightmare.

But it was too late to back out now. We were already in the areaway and Brains was at the window of the Curio Shop.

"Brains, we couldn't open that window last time we were here," I whispered hopefully. "It's probably locked. Maybe we'd better forget it!"

"The lock was unfastened," came the soft reply. "I checked when we were inside the store with Devlin."

See what I mean? Maybe Devlin didn't think much of Brains, but X hadn't missed a trick.

"Stay out in the alley and keep an eye on the street," he ordered. "I'll try to get this window frame open."

I heard the scraping of his pocket knife around the window frame as he tried to loosen it. Then came a rasping noise and I knew the window was open.

"All set!" Brains whispered, and beckoned to me.

I could see the opening of the window. If you think the alley was dark, you should have seen the inside of that shop. It was blacker than the inside of a tar barrel at midnight.

Brains hopped up on the sill and threw a leg over.

I made a last-minute appeal. "Brains! Wait! How do we know Silas is gone? Maybe he's still in there—just waiting for us! Maybe Devlin and Whisper are there too! Suppose it's an ambush?"

"You may be right," said Brains, "but we'll never find out for sure just waiting here. Let's go!"

Scared as I was, I followed him in. Creeps! It was better than waiting in that alley alone.

Brains led the way past the stacks of boxes, barrels and assorted junk. "Hang on to me," whispered Brains.

Hang on! He couldn't have pried me loose with a crowbar.

We were following the faint beam of the flashlight but the batteries were getting weaker by the second. The cone of light began to fade away.

And then suddenly *it was gone!* We were in complete darkness!

"Brains," I whispered, "where are you?"

"Right here, Operative Three," came the answer. "You're holding on to my zipper jacket."

I was, too!

"For Pete's sake, where are we? How do we get out of this place?" I was stupefied with fear.

"Relax, Jimmy, you're right next to the work bench. Just hold on for a minute. I know where to find a light."

How he could tell where to find anything in this king-size booby trap was beyond me. But a second or two later, Brains struck a match and lit a small candle stub.

"Holy cow! How'd you know where to find those matches— and the candle?"

"Elementary," Brains replied. "I noticed them on the workbench when we were in here last. But this is no time for quiz games. We will proceed with the investigation."

Yes, sir. Old bird-dog Benton was on the job!

"Okay," I said. "Just what are we looking for and how do we go about finding it in this gosh-awful mess?"

"If my guess is correct, we should find some partly finished coin dies somewhere around here," replied Brains. He began to open the drawers under the bench.

Rummaging through the drawers he kept mumbling to himself in that zany way he does whenever he's following a hot trail. But all he found was a collection of files, chisels, and a lot of needle-sized tools.

He was working on the bottom drawers when suddenly he let out a yelp! "Got something, Jimmy!"

"Let's see it," I gasped. My heart did a double somersault.

He lifted a small, heavy wooden box onto the bench. It was jam-packed with face tissues. There, resting inside, were two halves of a coin die.

We'd hit pay dirt!

"Creeps!" I said, "what kind of a coin would that be for? It must be the size of a silver dollar."

I tried to make out the design in the flickering candlelight. One side of the die had a group of horses pulling a chariot. There was something that looked like an angel floating over it. The other die face showed the head of a woman with three fishes swimming around near the edge of the design.

"Brother, this is it!" I said. I couldn't feel better if we had found a diamond mine. "All we have to do is bring this to the police and they'd grab Gorme so fast—"

"Yes, and the rest of the gang would be out of town by morning," said Brains. "Remember, this die only implicates *Gorme*. There's no proof against the rest of the gang. We couldn't even tell the police where to find them."

"Once Gorme was nabbed," he added, "Devlin and the others would know the jig was up and run for it."

Brains pondered the dies. "No, we must continue our investigation. We won't call in the police until we have this case wrapped up to present to the jury."

"But this die is important evidence," I said. "If we leave it here, we can't prove we ever saw it."

"Never fear, Jimmy, I intend to have an accurate copy of that design before I leave."

Putting the candle down, Brains wiped the faces of the dies with an oily rag. Then he tipped the candle over the dies so the drippings filled the hollows of the design.

"What gives?" I asked.

Brains was too busy to answer me. With the point of a pen-knife he was lifting the solid blob of wax from the top of the first die. It came away a little misshapen, but the image was clear—four horses, a chariot, and an angel flying overhead.

"There you are, Jimmy, a clear wax impression of the design," said Brains, as he began to peel the wax from the second die.

"Terrific!" I said. "I'd never have thought of using the candle that way!"

"An investigator must learn to adapt himself to every situation," Brains said. He took a quick look at his watch. "Almost nine o'clock. We've been here an hour."

That bit of news gave me the heebie jeebies.

"Holy smoke! Silas might be coming back any minute. Suppose he catches us here!"

"We'd better see that he doesn't," said Brains.

He wrapped the dies and slipped them back into the drawer. Then Brains blew out the candle. I heard him putting the stub down somewhere. Silas would find it exactly where he left it.

"Great!" I said. "Now, how do we find our way out of here in the dark?"

It was a foolish question. Brains was like a seeing-eye dog. All I had to do was latch on to his zipper jacket and he guided me right back to the window.

We were about to slip through into the areaway when suddenly there was a rattling noise at the front of the shop.

"Gorme!" snapped Brains. "He's at the door! Quick, through the window!"

As if he had to tell me! Brother, I streaked out of there like a scalded cat!

I was halfway up the alley when I realized something was missing.

*That something was Brains Benton.*

I knew right then he must have fallen somewhere in the area-way. Maybe he was hurt. The thought of going back put me in a blind panic. But I just couldn't leave Brains in the lurch.

I headed back into the dark!

# 17 THE CROOKED TRAIL

I don't know what I expected to find back in that tunnel of horror, but as I went back my knees were turning to jelly.

I nearly collapsed when Brains met me at the areaway.

"Brains! For Pete's sake, what happened?" I whispered.

"*Somebody* had to close the window, Operative Three."

That shook me! An open window would have given everything away. The finger would have pointed straight at us!

Just then a light snapped on inside the shop.

"Come on," Brains whispered. "Let's go!"

We did.

We picked up our bikes at the end of the alley and headed for the Turnpike. Fifteen minutes later we were at my house.

"Report for duty right after breakfast," Brains commanded. "There is much work to be done."

Wouldn't you know it? There he was giving me orders like a general again. He didn't have to tell me when to report. With this case breaking wide open, I'd be ready for action at the crack of dawn.

But the next day when I reported for duty, Brains had been working at the case for hours. As I entered the lab, he was pounding away at the typewriter.

"There," he said as he finished, and yanked the paper free, "that's done."

He turned and handed the paper to me. "Here, Jimmy. This is the formal report to our client on the Dexter case."

I read it briefly. He had everything down all right. How we overheard Devlin and Gorme. And all about our special investigation of Gorme's shop and how we found the dies. But the skimpy way he wrote about it, it didn't sound like much at all.

"Brother," I said. "All we went through and you cut it down to a paragraph!"

"I purposely kept it brief," Brains said. "We have a great deal to do today. As a matter of fact, I've got a special mission for you."

I perked up. A special mission! That was more like it!

"Just tell me what it is," I snapped. "Anything you say."

"I want you to deliver that report to our client, Terry Dexter, personally."

That floored me! Some special mission!

"What am I around here? Just an errand boy?" I demanded. "How about you doing some of the routine work?"

"I have a most important assignment to cover myself," said Brains, frowning.

He moved to a table loaded with open books. Lying close by were the two wax impressions Brains had made from the dies.

"I'm trying to trace the new coin Devlin and Company are planning to mint. But I find my father's library sadly deficient on the subject of numismatics. I'm afraid I'll have to consult the reference room of the Crestwood library. I may be there for hours. Still, we are pressed for time and the investigation must proceed. That's why you must go to Bleeker City."

"What's so important about me delivering that report to Terry?" I demanded.

"That will only be part of your mission, Operative Three," he said. "You're to ask Terry for as many coin catalogues and trade journals as she can spare. I want to check them for any news of counterfeiting activity."

Well, *somebody* had to do the leg-work. I folded the report and slipped it into a pocket.

"Okay, Chief," I said, "I'll get started right away."

"Just one more thing," he said, leaning back in his seat and looking at me over his glasses. "Do you recall Devlin mentioning some supplies that would be shipped in?"

"Right," I replied. "Gorme said he had already received a shipment and delivered it to the plant. That must have been the heavy package we saw him get from the postman."

Brains nodded. "It's important that we find out what *kind* of supplies are being shipped, and *where* they come from. I'm depending on you to get that information."

"That won't be easy," I said, frowning. "I could ask questions at the Bleeker City Post Office, but they might bounce me out on my ear."

"How you get the information is immaterial! But get it! I have full confidence in you, Operative Three."

He put his hand on my shoulder. Brother, I felt my chest expand a good six inches.

"Okay, Brains," I said, "I'll get the information." I'd get him the keys to Fort Knox if he wanted them.

He wished me luck. I had an idea I would need it.

But when I arrived at the Dexter store in Bleeker City, I found the door locked and a sign that read:


CLOSED ON ACCOUNT OF ILLNESS


That meant that Jeremy Dexter had had another one of his attacks. Good grief! This case must have hit him pretty hard. In a lower corner of the sign was a small note which read:

In emergency please call
Jeremy Dexter
335 Ramsey Drive

Well, I'd have to go over to Terry's house to deliver the report and get the catalogues and magazines. But for Pete's sake, where was Ramsey Drive?

I was about to stop a passer-by, when all of a sudden someone tapped me on the shoulder.

"Hi, Jimmy," said a hearty voice behind me. "What are you doing here in Bleeker City?"

I turned. It was Officer Burney!

When I told him I was looking for Terry, he grinned. "Glad to see you two became friends. It's better that way."

"It sure is," I agreed. Just thinking about Terry's left hook made my teeth ache.

Anyway, Burney showed me how to get to Ramsey Drive, and a few minutes later I was handing the report to Terry.

I found her outside the Dexters' one-story shingle house. She was busy setting out some bulbs. Her father was nowhere in sight.

She was tickled to see me. But the report was what really amazed her.

"You mean Mr. Devlin is the head of a counterfeiting gang? I just can't believe it."

"That's the trouble," I said. "Hardly anyone else will believe it either, unless we prove the case to the hilt. That's the main reason I'm here. Brains and I want you to help us."

I told her about the coin catalogue and trade magazines Brains needed—and two minutes later she brought me a stack of them from the house.

"Dad's asleep now," she said. "He's resting and he looks a lot better than he did yesterday."

I tied the stuff she gave me to the rack on the back of my bike. Then I asked her how to get to the post office.

And that's where I made my mistake. Terry was on the ball! Right then she guessed what I was up to.

"You're going to check on those packages Gorme's been receiving!" she said.

Brother! Did she score a bull's-eye.

"How did you guess?" I demanded.

"That package Gorme got two days ago looked pretty suspicious to me, so I've been doing a little investigating myself," she explained. "Mr. Fromber, the postman, delivers our mail, too. He told me Gorme gets packages like that all the time. But when I asked where the parcels came from, Mr. Fromber said it was all private information. So, if you're planning to question Mr. Fromber—"

"Uh-uh," I shook my head. "Not after you messed things up. He'll get suspicious the minute I mention Gorme's name."

Terry snapped her fingers. "Got it! . . . Maybe we could find out what we want from Miss Finch, the postmistress."

"Where do you get the we-stuff?" I asked. "I'm going to handle this *myself*, without any interference from you."

"Me, interfere?" she said innocently. You could almost see a shining halo around her head. "I wouldn't dream of doing that. I'll just show you the way to the post office. I've got to go there anyway . . . to buy a few blocks of that new Park Memorial stamp that was just issued . . . for the store, you know."

Well, I couldn't stop her from coming along, so I'd just have to make the best of it.

When we got to the Bleeker City Post Office, we parked our bikes and went in. "Just remember," I warned. "Let me do the talking, Terry. I don't want you gumming things up."

"Okay, okay!" she said. "Handle it your way!"

The Bleeker City Post Office wasn't much different from the one in Crestwood. There was a bank of letter boxes standing about six feet high with little combination dials on each of them. And smack in the middle was a double window where you bought stamps and money orders.

I walked up to the window with Terry beside me. Looking through, I could see a little old lady wearing glasses—the old-fashioned kind that pinch on your nose, with a long ribbon dangling from the corner.

Her hair was yellowish gray and kind of wispy and loose. You got the idea she pinned it up in a real neat bun every morning, but it became undone before long.

She was sorting letters into the backs of the mail boxes, flitting from box to box like a little gray butterfly.

"That's Miss Finch, the postmistress," whispered Terry.

Miss Finch must have heard her. She came over to the window. "Why, *hello,* Theresa! And how is your dear father?" she twittered.

"Much better, Miss Finch," said Terry. "Thanks."

"Oh, how *nice!*" beamed Miss Finch, fluttering back to her letter boxes. "Just a moment, dear, I'll be right with you."

Then, suddenly, I heard her voice again. But it came from the *opposite* side of the window.

"Why hello, Theresa, how are you, my dear? And how is your dear father today?"

I did a double-take. It was Miss Finch all right. You couldn't mistake that wispy hair and those glasses. Only this time I noticed that she was wearing one of those hearing-aid buttons in her ear.

"Oh, hello, Miss Finch," answered Terry. "Dad's much better, thank you."

"That's nice," said Miss Finch, darting up to the window with a foggy smile and a batch of letters in her hand, as if she'd just seen us for the first time. "And is there something I can do for you, my dear?" she asked.

"Why yes," said Terry. "May I have four blocks of the new Park Memorial stamps, please."

"Of course," said Miss Finch. "Wait right here, while I get them from the safe." And away she swooped.

Brother! I thought. Now I've seen them all.

I turned to Terry. "Say, what's with her? Didn't she hear what you said the first time she asked about your Dad?"

"Of course," said Terry.

"Then, why'd she ask you about him the second time?"

Before Terry could answer, there was that giddy old lady bouncing back to us from the other side of the window. Only this time she'd taken the hearing aid *off*.

"I'm sorry, Theresa dear, but somebody will be along to help you in a minute." And away she went.

Good grief! What was going on here? That old lady had my head spinning like a top.

And then all of a sudden, I was seeing double. Because there they were—*two* of them! And both of them were Miss Finch. Only one of them was sorting mail and the other one, with the hearing aid, was fishing a batch of stamps out of the safe.

That was when it hit me. "Hey," I said. "They're twins!"

"Of course," said Terry, giggling. "And they're both Miss Finch, too. The one sorting the mail is Amantha. The other one's Corintha. They dress alike, so it's hard to tell them apart."

"Not so hard," I said. "One of them wears a hearing aid."

Amantha stopped sorting mail and flitted over to the window again. "You're wrong, young man," she said. "That's not a hearing aid at all, it's a radio. Corintha just dotes on classical music. Listens to it *constantly!* And what was it *you* wanted, young man?"

I stood there with my mouth open. Those two zany characters had made me forget completely. I felt as daffy as I thought they were. I'd still be standing there if Terry hadn't interrupted.

"He wants to ask some questions, Miss Finch."

"Questions? Oh *my!*" said Amantha in delighted surprise. "Are you taking a poll, or making a survey?"

That was when I remembered that I was here to find out about those mysterious packages Silas Gorme was receiving.

I had a *Daily Ledger* subscription pad in my pocket. I whipped it out pretending that it was a notebook.

"I'm from a newspaper, Miss Finch. Er—the *Crestwood Daily Ledger!*"

Well, it wasn't a lie! I *was* from the *Ledger*—even if I only had a delivery route!

"We were planning an article about the faraway places which send mail to Bleeker City," I said, thinking fast on my feet.

"Why that sounds perfectly thrilling," Corintha cut in. She handed the stamps to Terry and took the money.

"A fascinating idea," said Amantha. "Why yes, we do get letters from distant places. Only last week I saw one from the Eskimo country, a place called Keokuk!"

"*Amantha!* Keokuk is in the United States," scolded her sister. "Why don't you tell him about Mr. Fourier, the hairdresser, and the letters he gets from Paris."

Well, I had them started on the grand tour. London, Paris, New Zealand . . . It looked like Bleeker City folks had contacts everywhere on earth.

We were making our second trip around the world when I realized I still hadn't found out about Gorme's packages. It was time to change the subject.

"Tell me, Miss Finch," I asked, not caring which Miss Finch answered. "What were the heaviest packages you ever received? Our readers would like to know."

"Oh," said Amantha, "we get sets of encyclopedias—"

"And sometimes plants and bushes," interrupted Corintha.

"How about *small* packages?" I interrupted, trying to steer the conversation closer to where I wanted it. "I'll bet you get some *small* packages that are *mighty heavy*."

Terry grinned. She knew just what I was fishing for.

"Well, let me think," said Amantha, thoughtfully. "Some small parcels *can* be quite heavy for their size. Those packages Mr. Gorme gets from all over the country. You know, the man who runs the Curio Shop!"

I stopped breathing. This was like picking a winning ticket in the sweepstakes.

"As a matter of fact," she continued, "one of those packages was so heavy it slipped out of my hand."

"Smashed to bits, I'll bet," said Terry, hopefully excited.

"Well no," said Amantha. "There was nothing breakable inside."

That was when Corintha rejoined the conversation. "No, nothing broke! But oh, my! You should have seen the coins scatter across the floor! Why, there must have been *hundreds* of them."

"Come to think of it," interrupted Amantha, "I just found one of those coins this morning when I swept under the safe."

My eyeballs nearly popped out!

"Do you mind if I see it, Miss Finch?" I begged. "I'm interested in old coins."

That was no lie, believe me!

"Of course," chirped Amantha. She opened a drawer and took out a silver piece, big as a quarter. It had the face of a woman with a mess of hair that looked like snakes engraved on it.

Brother, if I only had had a candle, I could copy it the way Brains did.

Then all of a sudden I had the answer!

"Please, Miss Finch, I'd like to make a rubbing of that coin, if you don't mind."

"A *rubbing?* And just how do you do that?" asked Amantha.

I ripped a page out of the subscription book, laid it across the coin and rubbed the side of my pencil point lightly up and back across the paper. In a second you could see the design rubbed into the paper in black, something like a picture negative.

"Oh, my! How very clever you are," breathed Amantha. I didn't disagree.

I turned the coin on its other side and got a rubbing of the other face.

I grinned at Terry and she grinned right back at me. We had it made.

I folded my notebook importantly and stowed it in my pocket.

"Well, thank you, ladies, I think I've got enough information now."

"Please come back soon, young man," called Amantha as Terry and I headed through the door.

"Yes, do," Corintha said.

Outside the post office, Terry Dexter grabbed me by the arm. "Did you hear that?" she asked breathlessly. "There were hundreds of coins in that package. But if Gorme and Devlin are counterfeiters, what do they need those coins for? I don't get it!"

"Of course, you don't," I said. "That's because you're not a trained investigator."

I hopped on my bike and tore off, leaving Terry with her mouth wide open in indignation.

But if you want the truth, those coins had me stumped too. Here I'd spent all this time finding out what was in those packages Gorme was receiving. And now that I knew, I was more confused than ever!

# 18 THE CLUE

I made the trip back to Crestwood in record time. By now my bike could have traveled the road by itself.

As I climbed up the secret stairway into the lab, I expected to find Brains hard at work. Instead I found the lab in complete darkness.

"Brains," I said, "where are you?"

I heard something moving in the dark. There was a faint click and the lights came on. Brains was standing there fiddling around with a camera and flash gun.

He was turning the film winder as if he'd just finished taking a shot.

I didn't get it. I hadn't seen the flash gun go off. And how could anyone possibly take a picture in the pitch dark?

"All right, Brains, let's have it. What's with the camera?"

He put the camera down and smiled.

"An experiment in photography," he said. "I shall explain it to you in due course. But at the moment we have more pressing affairs. Kindly present your report, Operative Three."

I filled him in on the events in Bleeker City while he took rapid notes for the Dexter file.

"Operative Three," he said, as I finished, "you have carried out your mission in an exemplary manner. But now comes the problem of putting all the pieces of the puzzle together."

He picked up the rubbing, the catalogues and the magazines from Terry, and carried them all to a table.

I could see some of the titles on those heavy volumes: *The History of Coin Collecting, Famous Counterfeiters of History* and three or four others like that.

For the next few moments he was thumbing through the catalogues with the rubbing in his hand, muttering to himself. Here and there he made a pencil check. Then he tackled the pages of the trade magazines.

Suddenly I knew he'd found what he was searching for. Because he snapped his fingers and put a paper marker in-between two pages. Then he picked up the wax impression that he had made in Gorme's shop the night before.

"This impression is the copy of one of the most beautiful coins in the world. The original was minted in the Greek colony of Syracuse, twenty-five hundred years ago."

He pointed to the chariot on the design. "This chariot signifies the great victory of Syracuse over Athens in 412 B.C. On the other side of the coin we see the Nymph Arethusa surrounded by dolphins."

"Uh-huh," I said. "Easy now, Brains. You're beginning to sound like your father."

Brains smiled. He knew just what I meant. His dad was a professor of ancient history and many a time he'd nearly put us to sleep with his stories of battles that no one ever remembered any more.

"Very well, Operative Three, we'll get down to the facts. Those dies we found in Gorme's workbench are designed to copy the silver Decadrachm of Syracuse. *Specimens of that coin are worth eight hundred dollars or more!*"

I let out a long whistle. "Brother, if Devlin and his bunch run off a couple of hundred of these they could clean up!"

"And that is precisely what they will do," said Brains. "Unless we can stop them."

He picked up the rubbing I'd made. "These coin shipments by mail proved puzzling, but I think I have the answer."

He turned to the volume labeled, *Counterfeiters of History*.

"According to this book, counterfeiters often got the raw material for their spurious coins by melting down similar, but less valuable, pieces."

I jumped up. "Hey! That's *it!* The gang is going to melt those shipments down in order to mint far more valuable counterfeits!"

Brains nodded. "My guess is that they plan to go into production of this rare decadrachm as soon as the dies are finished."

"Holy cow! Brains, this counterfeiting outfit must be really big if they can organize things like this," I said.

"Bigger than you think, Jimmy! Here, read this article in the *Coin Collectors Quarterly*."

I did. It started out with bold, black headlines:

#### NUMISMATICS SOCIETY WARNS COLLECTORS OF FRAUDS

The article said the country was being swamped by a flood of fake ancient Greek and Roman coins—so perfect in detail that only experts could detect them. The country's finest collections were being ruined.

"Just think of it, Jimmy," said Brains, pacing up and down indignantly. "Almost five thousand people become coin collectors each year. Beginners with little knowledge of the field. Counterfeiters like Devlin are having a field day swindling them out of millions."

"But with the information we have, we can stop them cold!" I said, enthusiastically. "All we have to do is go to the police."

Brains regarded me sourly. "That would be a trifle premature. For the present, Benton and Carson are handling the case with the highest skill and efficiency. The authorities will be informed only after we have *all* the details of the gang's operations."

"*All* the details! What more do we need? We've checked every angle there is!"

"We have not yet discovered the scene of their major activities. The place they call the 'plant'!"

"For Pete's sake, Brains!" I said. "We don't even know how to begin looking for it. You yourself admitted it might take days to locate."

"I have a simple solution to the problem," he said. "We only have to follow Silas Gorme the next time he delivers a shipment of coins to the plant."

I had a hard time swallowing. "You're not serious about tracking that gang right into their hideout?"

From the stubborn set of his jaw, I didn't have to see his nod to know that his mind was made up.

"Hey!" I almost yelled. "You've got rocks in your head. Devlin may have a dozen men at the plant. We'll be stepping into a cage of lions!"

"Lion tamers do it all the time," he commented.

That did it! Right then and there I told him I didn't want any part of it.

I'd followed him through the window of the Curio Shop in the dead of night. I'd risked getting caught eavesdropping outside of Devlin's office. I was ready to take any reasonable gamble. But no one was going to brainwash me into risking my life against a whole gang of crooks on their own home ground.

If Brains wanted to go, he was welcome to. I wasn't having any.

When I got it all off my chest, I left headquarters—and Brains didn't even try to stop me.

I came home and had my lunch. It was my favorite, a roast-beef sandwich with dill pickles. I told myself I was enjoying it, but I choked on every bite.

I was still boiling when I started on my paper route that afternoon. Usually I'm a perfect shot with a folded copy of the *Ledger*. But that day I couldn't hit the side of a barn. Time after time I had to stop my bike to retrieve a newspaper from under a porch or from the top of a bush.

I threw Mr. Bates' *Ledger* in the fish pond and had to give him another. And old lady Rader's paper landed up in her climber roses. She made me get a ladder and bring it down. Believe me, the thorns on those roses didn't do my temper any good either.

I came home to supper grumpier than ever. My parents and Ann were all in a dither about some letter Ann had received from Camp Avon. It was a summer camp for teen-agers that specialized in dramatics. Ann had applied for a working scholarship. There hadn't been any openings but, just today, Ann had received word that one of the scholarship students had dropped out and she had to report for an interview the next day.

"Oh, Jimmy, isn't it exciting?" said Ann. "Dad's taking the day off and he's driving Mother and me up to the camp."

"I thought you might want to come along," said my father, "but then I remembered your newspaper route."

I guess I was supposed to look excited and act interested, but I had more important things on my mind. And I couldn't have cared less.

As a matter of fact, I kept mumbling and talking to myself through most of the meal until my father said, "What's wrong, Jimmy? You attacked that lamb chop as if it were a deadly enemy."

"And for pity's sake," added my mother, "who's this person you're mumbling about that keeps bossing you around and giving you orders?"

"Oh," I said gloomily, "it's nothing important." I excused myself and rose from the table.

Dad and Mom looked at each other in surprise when I stayed home to watch television after supper, but I didn't care.

There wasn't very much on that night, just a lot of ancient movies I'd seen a dozen times. I watched without paying the slightest attention.

I kept thinking of Brains going down to the place they call the plant and facing that gang alone. Brother! He'd get the going over he was looking for if they caught him snooping. They'd clobber him, but *good!*

Yes, I could see it as if it was right in front of me on television. There was Gorme, Devlin, Whisper and maybe half a dozen other men crowding in on Brains. Then I saw X battling with his back to the wall. Alone! Deserted by the friend he had depended on. In my imagination I saw Brains going down, fighting to the last!

What a pal I was to let a friend face such odds alone. *How chicken can you get?*

I shot up out of my seat and headed for the phone in the hallway.

But even before I could touch it, the phone rang.

I grabbed it!

It was Brains!

"Jimmy," he said and stopped, his voice sounding strained.

"Brains," I said anxiously. "Something's wrong! What's happened?"

"Everything's all right, Jimmy," was his reply. "It was just that I've been thinking over what you said. Maybe you were right about the mission to the plant being dangerous . . . Anyway, it isn't worth losing your friendship over something like that. I'm ready to turn the case over to the authorities."

I heard what he was saying all right, but I couldn't believe it.

"*What?*" I sputtered. "After I stick with you through thick and thin, here you are ready to give up the case just when we're about to solve it! Brains, I'm *ashamed* of you."

"But Jimmy, you said . . ."

I cut him off. "Never mind what I said! You don't have to give in every time I put up a beef, do you?"

"Wait! You really mean that?" asked Brains excitedly.

"You're darned tootin'!"

"Very well, Operative Three," his voice crackled. "Please

report to headquarters at nine tomorrow, and try to be prompt for once!"

"Yes, *sir!*" I said, and hung up.

Man! Did it ever feel good to have Brains his old self again.

Getting started for headquarters early the next day wasn't easy.

First Mom gave me special instructions about what to eat for lunch. Then she gave me orders about the roast in the refrigerator, and when to put it in the oven, so supper would be ready by the time they got back from Camp Avon.

It was after nine when they waved good-by and drove toward the Turnpike.

A second later Brains came rolling up on his bike. He carried a pair of binoculars in a shoulder case. I started to explain about Ann and the folks but he didn't even hear me. You could see he was sore because I hadn't shown up at headquarters.

"We haven't a moment to lose, Operative Three," he snapped. "If we're going to be at Gorme's shop when the mailman comes."

Creeps! He was right! We'd have to burn up the Turnpike to make it! And we did!

We weren't sure Gorme would get a parcel that day. But our gamble paid off. Just as we came up Gorcey Street we saw the mailman entering the Curio Shop.

"This may be it," said Brains.

It was! Silas emerged right behind the mailman. He had a package in his hand. And a minute later he was driving off in a battered old car that had been standing at the curb.

"Let's go!" Brains ordered. "But don't crowd him. He mustn't know he's being followed!"

There's a fifteen-mile-an-hour limit in Bleeker City so it wasn't hard to keep up with Gorme, especially since he took a lot of bumpy back streets. But as soon as we were out of town, Gorme began going fast.

That heap of his sure could travel. Each time he went over a rise we lost sight of him. That's when we started pumping those pedals as if our lives depended upon it. But the gap between us kept getting larger.

Then all of a sudden, as we hit the top of a low hill, he was gone! The road stretched ahead of us for miles, *but Gorme was nowhere in sight!*

# 19 THE MYSTERIOUS WARNING

"What's happened?" I sputtered. "He just vanished into thin air."

That's when Brains grabbed a look with his field glasses.

"Jimmy," he ordered, "look down there! That house next to the grove of trees!"

I looked through the glasses. Just below, at the bottom of the rise, was a clump of trees right near the side of the road. Through the tree tops you could make out the shape of an old frame house, the big rambling kind with gables and porches. It lay on the other side of the grove, about a hundred feet back from the road. There was a yard in back and a couple of shacks. Beyond the shacks the woods began again, stretching out for a good quarter mile.

"Do you think Gorme could have headed in there?" I asked Brains doubtfully.

"He had to," was the reply. "There's no other building in sight. Come along, we'll check!"

We hopped off our bikes and wheeled them down the side of

the road by hand. If anyone was watching from the house, we'd be harder to spot that way.

It was a warm day, but as we moved closer to the house I felt chilled to the bone.

"For Pete's sake!" I whispered. "Are you going right up to the door and knock?"

Brains shook his head. We'd just about reached the grove of trees on our side of the house.

"Into the trees!" he snapped. "We'll leave our bikes here and crawl the rest of the way."

Before I could protest, Brains had leaned his bike against a tree and was slipping through the underbrush toward the house.

So what could I do but follow him? I couldn't let him go alone, could I?

That small patch of woods stretched for two hundred feet before it reached the side of the house, but to me it was more like two hundred miles.

Someone had used it as a rubbish dump. The ground was cluttered with old tires, empty paint cans, broken bottles and chunks of rotting lumber. It was all I could do to keep from getting cut up as I trailed after Brains.

By now my nerves were jangling like a fire alarm! If the gang were in that house, they might have a lookout posted. I kept wondering when somebody would let go with a rifle or shotgun. I caught up with Brains and pulled at his sleeve.

"How do we know this is the place?" I whispered. "It doesn't look like a plant to me. It looks more like a run-down, abandoned old shebang!"

"It may be run-down," came the answer, "but it's not abandoned! Look there!"

I followed the direction of his finger. Through the line of trees I could make out the back of the house. There was a narrow driveway between the grove and the old gray building. And just where that driveway hit the back yard, I could see the tail end of Gorme's car.

"Creeps," I said nervously. "You're right! Well, now that we know where he went, let's beat it!"

"Not before we have explored the terrain," Brains answered.

I could see his curiosity wasn't satisfied. And remembering what curiosity had done to the cat, I winced.

Brains moved up another few feet. He could have used his binoculars but he seemed to enjoy getting close to danger, the way a bullfighter likes to get close to the bull. I followed him, too scared to do anything else.

We could see most of the back yard now. There were two other cars parked there besides Gorme's. One was Devlin's red sedan, the other was a small pickup truck. Right behind them was a big shed with double doors that must have once been a carriage house.

From somewhere in the main house we heard a thumping noise, like a heavy weight dropping, again and again.

"A power press," Brains said into my ear. "For minting those counterfeits."

I nodded.

There was another sound, too, like an outboard motor. It turned out to be an electric generator in back of the building.

"They need it to make the current for running the press," whispered Brains.

A minute later I saw heat waves rippling over a small, tin smokestack sticking out of the back shed.

"Maybe that's where they melt down those coins," I suggested.

It turned out I could make some pretty good guesses, too, because just then Devlin and Gorme came out of the shed door. Behind them I could see a man, stripped to the waist, stirring something in a heavy metal pot that was set over a gas flame.

Close by I could make out the shadows of some of those big tanks—the kinds that hold oxygen and acetylene.

But right now we had our eyes on Gorme and Devlin. They were walking toward the driveway in our direction. We wriggled down deeper into the tall grass and weeds that sheltered us.

It would be a miracle if they didn't spot us. But their heads were lowered and they were talking so I felt sure we hadn't been seen.

"This shipment has given us enough to get started on that decadrachm, Gorme," Devlin was saying. "We should have the metal ready for the presses by tonight."

Gorme began getting into his car. He and Devlin had their backs to us. Brains yanked my sleeve and gestured in the direction of the bikes.

I got the message. We'd seen enough. It was time to get out of there.

We were easing back through the woods, when Gorme started his car and began rolling up the narrow driveway toward the main road.

I don't know how it happened. Gorme should have had his eyes on the driveway, but somehow he caught sight of Brains and me slipping through the grove.

At least that's what I figure happened. Because Gorme let go with a yell that you could hear for three miles.

Behind him the house and the shed seemed to explode as half a dozen men burst out into the open.

"Run!" yelled Brains. "Head for the bikes!"

Run? Right then I was flying!

For some reason I looked back for an instant. Gorme, in a panic, was trying to turn his car around in the narrow driveway. In an instant the rear wheels had plunged off the gravel and jammed into a ditch. I heard Devlin shouting indistinctly above the roar of Gorme's engine.

Someone was yelling, "Run! Run!" I think it was Brains but I wasn't quite sure. I was too busy streaking through those woods.

Old tires, tin cans, broken bottles—nothing could slow me down. That rubbish dump was like a cinder track to me and I was out to set a new world's record.

But guess who beat me to the finish line? Believe it or not, it was Brains Benton!

You've seen cowboys mount their ponies at the dead gallop. Well, any cowboy would have been green with envy to see us vault on those bikes and take off.

We hit that first hill like a couple of rockets from Cape Canaveral. We didn't stop till we reached the top.

That was when Brains jammed on his brakes.

"Of all the confounded stupidity!" he gasped, trying to catch his wind. "A pair of trained investigators panicking like that."

"I suppose we should have stayed around and waited to be invited to tea," I said.

But he wasn't listening. He had focused his binoculars on the house.

"They're not following us," he muttered. "It would be interesting to know why."

"Why don't we go back and see what's keeping them?" I suggested sarcastically.

He didn't answer. He just handed me the field glasses to see for myself. I did.

Brother, that was a sight. By hanging his car up in the ditch, Gorme had jammed the narrow driveway. Devlin's car and the pickup truck couldn't get through. Devlin was hopping mad and shaking his fist at Gorme, just about ready to hit him.

I handed the binoculars back to Brains. "A lucky break," I said. "Now, let's take advantage of it and scram."

We did.

All the way back to Bleeker City, Brains kept looking around at the landscape and watching the road signs. He was really concentrating and I knew that when he got through he'd be able to draw a map of our whole route, including every stone, tree, and bump in the road.

Creeps! I hope he didn't think we'd ever come back *this* way again.

Once we heard a car coming up behind us. Someone was

racing his engine and we heard him a couple of minutes before he passed us. We ducked off the road and into the bushes. If it were any of the gang, we didn't want them to spot us.

It was Devlin himself! We recognized the car. And Whisper was in there with him.

"That means they've pulled Gorme out of the ditch," Brains said.

"It also means they could have three cars out looking for us," I added. Just the thought of it raised goose pimples on my spine.

We didn't know for sure if they were hunting us, but we were too scared to use the Turnpike to get back to Crestwood. Instead we picked up Old York Road, which used to be the main route before the Turnpike was built. It didn't carry much traffic nowadays, and that suited us just fine.

"Brains," I said anxiously, just before we came to Crestwood, "do you really think Devlin's bunch recognized us?"

He didn't have to answer, because right about then we were at a spot where the old road cuts close to the Turnpike. That's when we saw Gorme's car roaring past, heading back to Bleeker City from Crestwood.

"Does that answer your question?" asked Brains.

It did.

It wasn't until we stopped outside my house that we got a real good look at ourselves. We were a ring-tailed mess. Crawling through that old dump heap in the woods near the "plant," had torn and muddied our clothes. And all that bicycling had covered us with dust and perspiration.

"See you later," I called to Brains. "I've got to go in and clean up. After that I promised my mother I'd fix supper."

"Very well, Operative Three, I'll contact you later and arrange a strategy conference for tonight." Brains hopped back on his bike and headed home.

After all that chasing around, a shower sure felt good. I could just feel myself relaxing. Sure, we had had a close call, but it was all over now.

After I cleaned up, I fixed lunch . . . a triple decker of bacon, cheese, chopped egg and pickle . . . the kind of sandwich I wouldn't dare put together if Mom were around.

I was just sitting down to eat when the phone rang.

Darn that guy Brains I thought! Probably another mission. Couldn't he at least have waited until I finished lunch?

I picked up the phone.

"Hello," said a voice. "Is this Jimmy Carson?"

I was suddenly alert. *It wasn't Brains.* It was a grownup's voice, but kind of muffled as if someone was trying to disguise his voice by speaking through a handkerchief.

"This is Jimmy Carson," I admitted. "And who is this?"

"A friend," said the disguised voice, breathing heavily. For a minute there I nearly recognized it, but not quite.

"You're a nice kid, Jimmy, but you're headed for trouble," said the mysterious voice. "Keep your nose out of that counterfeit coin business, or you'll get hurt . . . And stay away from that house outside of Bleeker City! This is your first and last warning. . . . *Try it again and you'll end up in the emergency ward!*"

There was a click, as the speaker hung up on the other end.

## 20 HIGH TENSION

I stared at the phone in my hand as if it were a coiled cobra about to strike. When I put it back in the cradle, my hand was shaking so much I nearly missed.

*That voice!* I couldn't quite place it, but I'd heard it before. It had to be Gorme or Devlin, or one of the gang. But no matter who it was, he meant what he said. Brother! I was in a jam! Up to my neck!

All of a sudden I wanted my Dad around, and my mother, and Ann. And they weren't here! They were somewhere up at Camp Avon, hundreds of miles away. But I was here—alone—at the mercy of some character with murder on his mind.

I grabbed the phone. I had to call Brains! I started to dial, but my fingers fumbled so much I got three wrong numbers before I got through. My one break was that Brains himself answered. I couldn't have talked to anyone else right then.

"Brains," I gasped, "I just got a phone call!"

He cut me off. "I know," he said. "I got one too. From the same party, undoubtedly."

He was talking cautiously, so I knew Mrs. Ray was somewhere in the background.

"I'm petrified!" I said. "What if he comes after us?"

"Don't panic, Operative Three," Brains said. But I could tell from the sound of his voice that he was having a job keeping his own teeth from chattering. "Just sit tight! I'm coming right over!"

He was at my door in a matter of minutes, but I made sure to look through the curtain and check before I let him in.

"Brains," I said, grabbing his arm, "those guys could murder us. We've got to tell our folks."

"We can't," he pointed out. "For one thing, your parents are up at the camp with your sister. For another, my Dad and Mother are on a shopping trip and will be gone all day."

"Brains," I pleaded. "We've got to tell the cops. That gang's sure to try some rough stuff!"

"I doubt it." He tried to sound sure of himself. "Or they wouldn't have bothered warning us. They're not exactly sure how much we know. I believe they just want to scare us off."

He wrinkled his brow. "However, danger is a distinct possibility and I suggest we'd better stay together for the rest of the day. If the situation becomes really grave, we'll notify the police."

"Thanks," I said. And brother, that came from the bottom of my petrified heart.

He stayed with me for the next couple of hours. But honestly, the way he kept pacing up and down didn't do my nerves a bit of good.

I was getting more jumpy by the minute when I suddenly remembered the roast my Mother wanted me to put into the oven. It gave me something to do.

I took it out of the refrigerator. It was already in the pan. All I had to do was slide it into the oven.

"I'll have to keep an eye on the clock," I said. "Mom told me it should take about three hours."

Brains stopped pacing and shot a glance at the gas range. "Why don't you just set that automatic timer?" he asked.

"Because it hasn't been working for more than a year," I replied. "The repairman's been here twice but couldn't fix it."

"Indeed!" said Brains, suddenly perking up. "If you'll just hand me a screwdriver perhaps I can remedy the situation."

Was I ever grateful for that broken timer. It was just the thing I needed to calm Brains down and save myself from nervous collapse.

I gave him the screwdriver. He had the timer apart in a jiffy. The top of the range was covered with little relays, terminals and stubs of wire.

Brains kept muttering to himself as he started to put the gadget together again. I couldn't help wondering if he knew what he was doing.

But honest to Pete! He got it working better than new. As a matter of fact, he even added something—a warning buzzer that sounded off to let you know the roast was done.

By the time he finished fooling with that timer, Brains had relaxed completely.

After that he went out on my paper route with me. Believe me, I wasn't anxious to go, but Brains pointed out that I couldn't hide in the house for the rest of my life. And anyway he was coming along to keep an eye on me.

I started out expecting to be ambushed at the first dark alley. But no one bothered us at all. At least not until Brains and I were crossing Cherry Drive.

That was when a car shot down the street and headed straight for us. We barely made it to the sidewalk.

It was a *red sedan!*

I was sure it was Devlin at the wheel—until the car backed up and a friend of my mother's, a Mrs. Anderson, stuck out her head and apologized.

"I'm sorry, Jimmy," she said. "I stepped on the brake when I saw you, but the car just seemed to pull out from under me."

"That wasn't the brake you stepped on," explained Brains, in a strangled voice. "That was the accelerator!"

He was still shaking as Mrs. Anderson thanked him and drove away.

Well, that was the low point for both of us. After that we began to get our nerve back. I even went down to Bleeker City to deliver a *Ledger* to the Barnes'.

It was about six-thirty when we got back to my house. By then I'd just about forgotten about being afraid. After all, we'd been wandering all around town for the past couple of hours and nobody'd tried any rough stuff on us. So, I figured Brains was probably right. The man who had called on the phone was just trying to scare us off.

Brains offered to come in, but I told him to go along home. After all, I expected my family home any minute.

I'd only just stepped inside the house when I knew there was something wrong. The whole house echoed with a rasping noise like a rattler about to strike. It seemed to come from the kitchen. I headed down the hall and forced myself to open the kitchen door.

I nearly fainted with relief. The noise came from the oven. The roast was done. Brains had fixed the timer perfectly!

And that buzzer had *fixed me!* I had the heebie jeebies all over again.

Ann and my parents should have been home hours ago! Here I was all alone. Suppose Devlin and his gang came to get me! They could finish me off right here, and no one would be the wiser. A thousand crazy thoughts like that whirled through my head.

I tried to calm down by reading the *Ledger*. But the front page carried a banner headline about a murder in the state capital. A great help *that* was!

By now it was seven. It would be getting dark soon and the folks *still* weren't here.

What if the mysterious man called again? What would I say?

What would I do? I could almost hear that muffled, menacing voice in my ear—threatening to put me in the hospital. My blood ran cold.

*Then, without warning, the phone rang!*

It hit me like an exploding bomb. It could only be the mysterious stranger to give me another warning.

Suddenly I was as mad as a hornet. This guy couldn't scare me. What did he think this was? No one was going to call me up and bully me right in my own house. The phone was ringing like mad when I picked it up. I never gave him a chance to speak.

"Look here, Mister! I don't know who you are, but . . ."

"Jimmy," a voice cut in—a voice I knew well!

"Dad," I yelped. "Where are you?"

"Is there anything wrong down there, Jimmy?" asked my father.

I should have told him straight out, but I didn't want to frighten him. I was looking for a way to begin.

"There was a phone call," I told him. "Some guy pestering me."

Dad cut me off. "Oh, I know who you mean. He's been calling all week trying to sell me some uranium stock. Don't pay any attention to him. Jimmy, we're up here at Cross River, about a hundred miles from home.

"Everything's all right, and Ann got the scholarship," Dad went on, "but we've had a little trouble with the car."

My heart sank. "You mean you're not coming home tonight?"

"The mechanic won't get the car parts until tomorrow. We're putting up at a motel. We should be on the road by ten tomorrow morning."

That meant I'd have to spend the night alone in the house! Right then I decided to spill the works. "Dad, *listen*," I began.

But that was when Dad handed the phone to my mother. I clammed up. I couldn't tell *her!*

"Jimmy," she said. "Be sure to fix a good supper for yourself.

Have some of the roast beef. By the way, how did it come out?"

"Oh, swell," I said.

Yep, the roast beef was done. And my goose was cooked, too!

"Good-bye, Jimmy," she said. "And don't worry."

"Good-bye," I said as she hung up.

I wondered if I'd ever see her again.

I looked out. It was dark. Suppose the gang found out I was alone. *Creeps!* For all I knew they probably had the lines tapped by now.

I was a sitting duck, just waiting for the end!

I grabbed for the phone and dialed the Benton number.

It was Brains' father who answered.

"Could I speak with Brains . . . er . . . Barclay, Mr. Benton? It's an emergency!"

"Why, of course, James," said Mr. Benton. "He's right here."

A second later I was telling Brains about my folks not coming home that night.

"I'm just too jittery to stay here by myself! Could you ask your folks to let me sleep in your house tonight."

Brains thought for a moment. "Why certainly, Jimmy. I shall make immediate inquiries."

There was a pause, and then I heard his voice echoing through the phone, but what he said flabbergasted me.

"Oh, Mother. Jimmy's parents are away tonight and he's inviting me to stay over with him. May I?"

"Invited you over?" I exploded. "Brains, you've got it all mixed up . . ." But Brains wasn't listening. Something was going on at the Benton house that I didn't understand.

And then Brains was on the phone again. "It's okay, Jimmy!" he said heartily. "Not at all! Glad to do it! I'll be over in a few minutes!"

Good gravy, I thought. What did that foxy redhead have up his sleeve now?

He arrived on a bike about fifteen minutes later, carrying an overloaded canvas camping kit.

"For Pete's sake!" I said, letting him in. "Did you come here to stay the night or are you moving in permanently?"

"I took only the barest necessities," he said.

"You got it all mixed up! I wanted to come to *your* house," I informed him.

"I realized that, Operative Three," Brains replied, putting the kit down. "But I decided against it. With no adult supervision or restrictions here, your house makes a much better base for tonight's operations."

*"Tonight's operations?!"* I said, stupefied. I had a horrible suspicion of what was coming next.

"Operative Three, I've just decided on our course of action. I propose that we go back to the plant tonight! We're going to clean up the case!"

# 21 HOUSE OF PERIL

"You're bats!" I wailed. "To go back after those guys threatened us is just plain suicide!"

"They won't be expecting us," Brains said. "They think they have us too frightened to make a move."

"And how right they are!" I said.

"Jimmy, listen!" Brains said eagerly. "If we crack this case, our names will be carved beside those of Sherlock Holmes and Arsene Lupin!"

"They'll probably be carved on a couple of tombstones in Crestwood Cemetery, first!" I groaned.

"Come, come," said Brains impatiently. "We'll be perfectly safe. I've brought all the necessary equipment for an undetected reconnaissance."

He dragged his canvas kit in from the hall and began to unpack it on the living room table. First to emerge were two pairs of old pajamas, smeared with streaks of yellow, green, brown and black paint.

"Our stalking suits!" Brains said.

He didn't have to remind me. We'd used the outfits to camouflage our movements before.

Brains next took out a belt from which hung a small camera and a flash gun.

"This camera is our most important piece of equipment," he said. "We're going to make a complete photographic record of the gang's operations."

"With flash equipment?" I asked. "If just *one* of those bulbs goes off, that gang will be after us like a wolf pack."

"Hold it, Jimmy! These flash bulbs give off infra-red light, invisible to the human eye. And the film in this camera is sensitive only to the infra-red spectrum. We will take those photographs without being detected."

I looked at him skeptically. "You don't really expect me to believe that?"

Brains didn't reply. He merely smiled and took out a photo.

It was a picture of me. I was just stepping into the laboratory after coming up the secret stairway. I was squinting as if trying to see in the dark.

"When did you take this?" I said suspiciously.

"If you don't know, you have just proven my point," replied Brains. "I photographed you by invisible light when you came up to headquarters the other day and found everything in darkness."

I nearly flipped! "Hey, this is terrific stuff," I said.

"Permit me to show you how it works," said Brains.

He did. I had my own camera and flash gun. And this one wasn't much different, except that the lens was a better one and was protected by a rubber cap.

"I've estimated the exposure and set the controls," he instructed me. "All you'll have to do is remove the lens cap, wind the film, shoot the picture and change the bulb."

"Say, that's great!" I said enthusiastically. "With this rig I could snap Devlin and his gang and they'd never know I was there. We can't miss!"

And then suddenly I stopped. Brains was grinning from ear to ear.

He had baited the hook and I'd swallowed it. Plus the line and sinker.

"I was depending on *you* to handle the camera, Jimmy," he said. "I will be busy with other observations."

"Okay, you win!" I said.

You just couldn't beat this guy. He could talk a rabbit into a tiger's cage.

Well, we loaded up and started for the plant. I was carrying the belt with the camera, and a shoulder bag with a dozen infra-red bulbs and extra film.

Brains was lugging the canvas kit with the rest of our equipment.

There wasn't any traffic on the road, and a bright moon lit up the Turnpike. So we made good time back to Bleeker City.

Brains led the way through the back streets. He seemed to have our route all memorized. As a matter of fact, the streets were starting to look familiar to *me* too. And then I suddenly knew why. We were on Ramsey Drive!

"Brains," I said, "this is the block where Terry Dexter lives. If she ever spots us!"

My warning was too late. A shrill whistle pierced the night —and darned near pierced my ears, too.

"Jimmy! Brains!" A freckled-faced whirlwind shot out of the shadows of the Dexter porch. Terry had us cut off!

"Hey! Where are you two going?" she asked excitedly.

Brains cleared his throat, trying to think up a phony story, but nobody was fooling Terry.

"I know! You're working on the case! Wait up! I'm coming along!"

Brains and I exchanged looks. We still remembered how Terry had nearly bungled up the works in the alley behind Gorme's shop. If she came along on this trip, the whole case could blow up in our faces.

"Hold everything, Terry," I stopped her. "This mission is no picnic. We can't have you tagging along when we're tangling with a dangerous gang of—"

Brains groaned. He looked at me as if I'd just stabbed him in the back!

I gulped. Me and my big yap! I'd let the cat out of the bag. Now we'd never be able to keep her from coming.

"Jeepers!" said Terry. She was hopping around as though she was on a pogo stick. "You mean there's a whole *gang* of them! You've just *got* to take me with you!"

"Not a chance," I snapped. "You're not coming!"

"Out of the question!" Brains backed me up.

And with that we took off. We left her glaring after us with that bull-terrier look.

Terry was a good kid and I hated to turn her down like that, but we just couldn't risk having her underfoot tonight.

Soon we were leaving the outskirts of Bleeker City. It was clouding up now, and getting harder to make out the roads, but Brains kept us heading in the right direction as if we were on radar.

Once or twice I caught him looking back over his shoulder. "I have a strange feeling that we're being followed," he said. "But I guess I'm mistaken."

Just the idea had my nerves twanging. There was trouble enough waiting for us up ahead without more trouble sneaking up from behind.

We had been pedaling for a while and I was beginning to wonder if we had lost the road, when suddenly I saw that familiar clump of trees below us. It was too dark to see the house, but we knew it was there. We hopped off the bikes and started walking.

Instead of leaving our bikes among the trees, we slipped down the road to the entrance of the driveway.

For a minute or two we crouched in the undergrowth while Brains tossed a rock into the driveway entrance. If Devlin had a guard posted, the noise that rock made would flush him out.

But the coast was clear, so we ducked across the driveway and dropped our bikes in the high weeds behind a large FOR SALE sign.

"This sign should prove an excellent marker. It will make it easier to find our bikes in case of emergency."

"Emergency!" I gasped. Why did he have to say things like that? "I thought there weren't going to be any emergencies."

He didn't answer. He was too busy hauling our stalking suits out of the canvas kit bag. After we slipped into them, we put on a couple of battered old hats. Next came the burnt cork on our faces to kill any possible reflection. We were ready!

It was only then that I realized the crazy thing we were about to do.

"Brains, this is our last chance to think it over," I whispered. "Let's go back while we're still in one piece."

"Are you a detective or a scared rabbit, Operative Three?" he demanded fiercely. "Maybe you'd better hand *me* that camera!"

"Oh no you don't!" I said. "You used that camera to bait me and get me to come here. You're not going to take it over now!"

Brains didn't say another word. He turned and began sneaking up the driveway. Behind him hopped that faithful scared rabbit, Operative Three.

We began working our way toward the house, dodging from tree to tree. It was a horrible experience. The moon kept ducking behind the clouds and then coming out again. When it got dark we couldn't see where we were going. When it got bright we were too scared to make a move.

But I stuck close to Brains and pretty soon we were up to the house. That's when we slipped across the driveway and began moving along the ditch. That ditch was a break. It guided us along the driveway even though everything was pitch black.

Brains put his lips to my ear. "Keep your head down. These

men are dangerous and probably armed. They may shoot first and ask questions afterward."

With this happy thought to inspire me, I followed him toward the back of the house.

It looked as if Devlin's men were working in the two back rooms. Weak rays of light spilled out from beneath partly drawn shades.

Brains touched my arm and signaled me to remain where I was. Then he ducked across the driveway to look into the windows. A second later he was back.

"You'll have to go right up to the window," he whispered. "You can't be more than ten feet away or we won't get a decent shot."

"Why don't we just go up and ask them to pose," I hissed, but I followed him toward the building.

Inside the first window I could see Devlin supervising a man working at a small press. The man was feeding a metal strip into the machine, which kept pounding out round discs.

Once in a while Devlin would pick up one of the discs and examine it closely.

"On your toes!" Brains whispered. He dug a sharp elbow into my ribs. "Get some shots of Devlin examining a coin. Show him in action!"

I took the picture. There was no flash. But when I went to change bulbs I burned my hand, so I knew it had gone off. I took another two shots and then moved on to the next window.

That's where I spotted Gorme. He was working with two men who were rubbing finished coins as they held them under magnifying glasses. In another corner a third man was dipping baskets of coins into a vat, and taking them out all discolored.

"Gorme is showing them how to finish up the coin," whispered Brains. "They're cleaning off the rough spots with steel wool and then oxidizing them to give them an aged look."

I tell you that redheaded genius had learned enough to go into the counterfeiting business himself.

I had taken two more shots through the second window when Gorme and Devlin began to move toward the rear door.

Brains yanked me back from the window and signaled me toward the back yard. We were rounding the corner of the house when the pair emerged and headed for the shed.

"I saw the proofs you struck of that decadrachm. It looks good, Gorme," said Devlin.

"Best job I've ever done," boasted Gorme. "But when are you going to give me a real cut? I happen to know the stuff you turned out here in the past year catalogued close to a million."

Brains grabbed my arm. Brother! *A million dollars!* Suddenly I felt weak around the stomach.

"Wait a minute, Gorme," Devlin said. "That's not clear profit. I've got to pay for those old coins we use as raw material. And after we mint the new stuff, I can only sell it a little at a time. Flood the market, and the dealers wise up."

They opened the door to the smelter shed.

Brains gave me another dig. We moved into the back yard and ducked behind a parked car. From there I took another three shots of the smelter operation while the shed door was open.

Geronimo! That sewed it up. Brains plucked at my sleeve. We were finished and it was time to take off!

The moon had gone under completely now. We couldn't see our hands in front of our faces. But we knew just how to get back to the road. All we had to do was to ease over till we found the ditch. After that we began to follow the ditch along the driveway.

So far, so good! We must have sneaked about halfway back to the main road when suddenly it happened!

Without warning, Brains slammed into someone in the dark! I slammed into Brains! And down we all went in a heap!

A shrill yelp exploded under me!

*"One of Devlin's men!"* snapped Brains, as he scrambled to his feet. "Quick! Make a run for it!"

# 22 ESCAPE IN THE DARK

I heard Brains sprint down the driveway and tried to follow.

But I couldn't. This guy Brains had knocked down had got his foot tangled in my camera belt. It was like being caught in a mess of flypaper. My heart was pounding. I was wondering when he was going to start shooting.

Then, all of a sudden, someone said, "Let me up! Let me up or I'll bash you!"

That voice! It was Terry Dexter!

I hauled her to her feet. This was no time or place to ask questions. I began pulling Terry in what I hoped was the direction of the road.

Doors were now slamming open behind us. Somebody was yelling for a flashlight. I ran even faster, jerking Terry along behind me.

All at once I could make out the big FOR SALE sign and I yanked Terry into the high grass behind it.

We could see Devlin's men coming up the driveway with flashlight beams shooting every which way.

[ 164 ]

"What happened to Brains?" I groaned, heartsick. "If they catch him, he's a goner!"

"Calm yourself, Operative Three," said a familiar voice close by. "If they catch me, it will be due to your loud and unnecessary conversation."

It was Brains! He was lying there in the grass, only a foot away. Man, was I relieved!

Back on the driveway someone was arguing with Devlin.

"I don't see anyone out here, Devlin," said a voice. "It's your imagination. You've been jittery ever since those kids came snooping around this morning."

"I don't know," came Devlin's reply. "I was sure I heard something. If I did hear those nosy brats, they probably headed through the grove. Come on, we'll take a look at the spot where they hid their bikes last time."

We heard them tearing through the brush, heading away from us.

"Now's our chance!" exclaimed Brains. "Let's get out of here. We can't get back the way we came. They've blocked us off. We'll have to head down the road and try to find some other way back to Bleeker City."

"What about Terry?" I asked. "How is she going to get back?"

"Rats!" said Terry. "Did you think I walked all the way from Bleeker City? I've got my own bike right here leaning against the sign."

I nearly fainted! If Devlin's men had come just a little closer, their flashlights would have spotted her bike sure as shooting! A dead giveaway!

Brother, did I want to tell her off! But right now the most important thing was to clear out fast!

And that's just what we did!

We had gone about a mile when Brains slowed up and turned to Terry.

"Of all the idiotic tricks!" he snapped. "For pity sakes, Terry, what made you follow us? They could have captured us all!"

"They didn't, did they?" commented Terry, innocently. "Besides, I only wanted to help. . . . Anyhow, I'm your client and I've got a right to keep up with the case, haven't I?"

You could see talking to Terry was a waste of breath. All Brains could do was swallow hard and get going again.

The moon came out from under, but it didn't help much. Brains began to look confused.

"Do you know which way we're going?" I asked Brains.

"Frankly, no," was his reply. "The only way to Bleeker City I know leads back past the plant."

"Oh, for goodness' sakes! Why all the commotion?" asked Terry. "Just follow me. I know all these back roads. I'll show you the way to Bleeker City."

We followed her—but nervously. With that girl's talent for trouble, she would probably lead us into a bomb-testing range.

But though Terry took us over a dozen rough and winding back roads, we ended up in Bleeker City, right in front of her house on Ramsey Drive.

"Well, good night, men," she said. "Guess you're mighty lucky I showed up, or you'd never have found your way back."

"Good night, Terry," said Brains. "And *thanks!*"

I guess you know how he meant that word "thanks!"

"Glad to help," she said forgivingly. "And any time you need me on this case, just let me know."

I was fishing around for some nasty crack when all of a sudden Terry began to giggle.

"For goodness' sake!" she gasped. "Go on home and take off those ridiculous Halloween getups you're wearing." And with that she ran into the house.

Brains and I looked at each other.

We were still wearing our stalking suits, and our faces were covered with burnt cork.

"Operative Three," said Brains, "you look like something that crawled out of a swamp!"

"And you," I said in turn, "look like forty miles of bad road!"

Then we ducked down a dark side street and yanked off our stalking suits and stuffed them in the canvas kit.

The burnt cork on our faces had to wait until we hit the culvert where Spring Creek passes under the Turnpike. But by the time we got back to Crestwood, Brains and I could pass for human beings again.

Boy! Was I glad when we pulled up in front of my house.

"Come on, let's park these bikes and hit the sack," I said. "I'm bushed."

Brains looked at the illuminated dial on his watch. "Surely you don't intend to retire at nine-thirty?" he asked in disbelief.

"*Nine-thirty?*" I said. "You mean all that just happened in an hour and a half? Heck! I thought it must be nearly twelve."

"The night is still young, Operative Three," he said. "We still have time to go to the laboratory and develop that infrared film."

Good grief! *The pictures!* I'd forgotten all about them. Believe me, I was as anxious to see how they turned out as Brains was.

So, moments later we were heading up the alley that ran behind the Benton property. The alley led to the rear of the garage which was the laboratory and headquarters for the firm of Benton and Carson.

From the garage entrance we could see the lights in the Benton living room.

"Brains," I said, "maybe we ought to tell your folks we're here."

"There's no point in disturbing my parents," commented Brains. "Especially since my father's in the midst of writing his new book on the Punic Wars."

"The Punic Wars! Creeps! I'll bet those old Greeks never saw the action we saw tonight," I remarked.

"Idiot!" snorted Brains. "It was the Romans and the Carthaginians who fought the Punic Wars!"

The conversation was getting out of my line. "Come on," I said. "Let's get with it. I want to see those pictures!"

We slipped in through the front door of the garage. As we

closed the door behind us, Brains turned and pressed a screw head in the door frame. He didn't have to tell me what that was for. I knew. He had switched on the automatic burglar alarm that guarded our headquarters.

Any intruder who tried to break in would cut an invisible beam of light and set off a warning buzzer in the lab upstairs.

"Brains," I said nervously. "You don't think Devlin's men would dare to—"

"Probably not, but there's no point in taking risks."

*Taking risks?!* For Pete's sake, what were we doing till now—weaving daisy chains?

I followed him up the stairway, swallowing my indignation. Up in the lab, Brains went to work. He removed the roll of exposed infra-red film from the camera. Then from beneath the table he hauled a chrome-plated machine, mounted on rollers.

I'd seen most of the gadgets in the lab by now, so this one was no news to me.

It was an automatic film developer and printer. Brains had built it out of a lot of surplus photographic equipment and old electrical parts. I'd seen him put it together. *Whew!* He had everything in there—from a heating element from an old broiler to an old motor from a vacuum cleaner. But it worked like a charm. You put the film negative into a slot at one end, added chemicals and developers, and in about half an hour the finished prints popped out of the other end.

I watched him switch off the light in the lab. I heard the rustle of paper in the dark. Then came a click, and the hum of a motor. The faint blue glow from a pilot light told me the machine was on.

When the lab lights came on again, Brains was standing at the machine adjusting different dials. From a table he picked up several bottles of chemicals and poured them into the machine through a chrome funnel.

I got a boot out of it. He reminded me of one of those old wizards in the Middle Ages!

"And now, we wait!" said Brains, as he wiped his hands on a paper towel. "The process should take precisely thirty minutes."

He walked over to a table and began taking notes from the book on famous counterfeiters. I tell you that guy didn't waste a minute of his waking hours.

To me that was the longest half hour I ever spent. The machine hummed and gurgled as chemicals swished around, motors cut in and out, and switches clicked.

Then, at last, I heard another loud and final click. A small bell *tinged* once; a red light snapped on.

Brains got up. "The pictures are ready," he announced. He looked at his watch and grumbled. "The timing is off by thirty seconds."

Then he opened a slide on the side of the machine and took out a batch of glossy papers.

"The photographs, Operative Three," he said, importantly, as he held them up for examination.

Hopping with excitement, I looked over his shoulder. That moment nearly gave me heart failure.

*The prints were completely blank!*

"Brains!" I squawked. "There's nothing on that film at all."

"I have already made that observation," he said.

He bent over the developing machine, checking the controls. Then from another slot he extracted a strip of transparent negative film. He held it to the light, looking for images.

The negatives were blank too! We could see clear through them like a glass window.

"I just don't understand it," he muttered to himself. "I conducted dozens of experiments. It couldn't happen!"

That really got my goat. I mean the way he said it—as if he were Einstein or Edison or somebody! And his inventions just couldn't miss!

I'd always wanted a chance to take him down a peg and this looked like the time.

"Well, it *did* work," I said, innocently, "didn't it? After all, it was an experiment in invisible light. So what do you expect? You got invisible pictures!"

"This is no time for levity," Brains snapped.

"You're darned tootin', it isn't!" I sounded off. "And I'm not laughing either. We risked our lives trying to get those pictures. Devlin and that gang would have killed us—and for what? Brains, if you're going to use those gadgets of yours, at least make sure they work."

As a dressing down it was a beauty. But Brains never heard a word of it.

. He was poking at the machine, turning dials and pressing buttons to start it and stop it, smelling at bottles of chemicals. Then suddenly snapping his fingers as if remembering something, he went over to the camera lying on a nearby table. He examined it minutely, adjusting the controls and tripping the shutter. Abruptly he stopped and stared.

"Operative Three," he said, tensely, "would you be good enough to step over here."

I did, wondering what clever alibi he'd use to cover up his mistake.

"Kindly examine the camera closely," said Brains.

I picked it up and looked it over.

"What's wrong?" I said. "The camera looks fine."

"The lens cap!" said Brains, darkly. "Kindly observe the position of the lens cap!"

"It's exactly where it belongs. Over the lens . . ." And then I stopped, horrified!

The rubber lens cap! I had never removed it to take the pictures. All the time we'd been sneaking around the plant, gambling with our lives to take pictures, the lens had been covered! No wonder the film had been completely blank!

"Brains! What can I say?"

What could I say? I'd said it all when I was giving Brains that dressing down. Now all I could do was stand there and feel sick.

Brains ran his fingers through his hair and took a deep shuddering breath. If ever a guy looked licked, it was Barclay Benton!

"I admit it was my fault," I said, "but what do we do now?"

"I don't know, Jimmy! I just don't know!"

That's when it happened.

Without warning, a buzzer sounded. Over on Brains' desk a red light was flashing off and on.

"The burglar alarm!" he hissed. "Someone's trying to get in through the front door."

I nearly flipped my wig! It must be Devlin—and his gang! They've followed us here!

"Grab a weapon!" snapped Brains, as he picked up a wrench. "We'll let them know they've been in a fight!"

# 23 LAST CHANCE

I looked around for something heavy that I could swing. There was only one thing available, the camera! Almost without thinking I pushed it into the bag with the flash bulbs and spare film. I hefted the bag. It would do! Heaven help the crook that I slammed with it.

Brains had already slid open the panel in the wall of the lab. He slipped through it. I followed, my legs feeling as if they were made of sponge rubber.

Neither of us spoke a word as we went down the folding stairs and then outside through the secret entrance. Brains sent me an unnecessary signal for silence.

He then began easing himself along the side wall of the garage toward the front. I was so close behind him I was breathing down his neck.

At the corner of the garage, Brains stopped. He seemed to be taking a deep breath. I saw him raise his hand, grasping the wrench. Only then did he sneak a look around the corner.

I don't know precisely what I expected him to do at that moment. But what he did do had the same effect on me as a pin jabbed into an inflated balloon.

Brains laughed.

I was a candidate for a career of cutting out paper dolls until I, too, looked around the corner of the building. For standing there was Brains' mother, Mrs. Benton!

"Barclay! Jimmy! For Heaven's sake! What are you doing here? I saw a light in the laboratory and came to investigate. I thought you were sleeping at Jimmy's house."

"We were, Mother," said Brains, thinking on his feet. "But we suddenly remembered we had an experiment to complete."

"Well, if the experiment is complete, I think it's time you boys were in bed."

"In a manner of speaking, everything *is finished!*" said Brains, looking at me.

Since it was so late, Mrs. Benton decided that there was no point in going back to my house and that I should bunk in the extra bed in Brains' room. He could lend me a pair of pajamas.

The way I felt I didn't much care where I slept. If I could sleep at all—after that boner I'd pulled.

To show you how wound up I was, it wasn't until we were up in Brains' bedroom that I realized I was still carrying the small canvas bag with the camera.

I dumped it on a chair in the corner of the room and began to undress. Brains tossed me a pair of pajamas from his drawer without a word.

"All right," I said. "Cut out the silent treatment. Maybe I should have let you handle the camera when you wanted to. But we all make mistakes."

Brains shook his head. "It's not all your fault, Jimmy. Besides, we're partners and we'll take the praise or blame together."

Well, at least he was still talking to me. I began to pull on the borrowed pajamas.

"Okay," I said, eager to keep the conversation alive. "What's our next step? Got any ideas?"

He was in bed and pulling up the covers. "Can't think of a *thing*, Jimmy. I guess I'm too tired. Maybe we ought to just turn it over to the police and trust to luck that they collar the gang."

"But gosh!" I said. "After all the work we did and the chances we took, the police would get all the credit."

Brains never even heard me. His eyes were closed and soon his regular breathing told me he was asleep.

I sat there thinking. I couldn't sleep a wink, I was that worried and jumpy.

It was all my fault. Here Brains had worked so hard solving the case. And now, just as he was about to clinch it, some lame-brain had fouled up the works!

If I could only make it up to him, I thought. If there was some way we could go back and do it all over again!

That's when I caught sight of the canvas bag with the camera. It was still lying on the chair near the window, where I dropped it when I came into the room.

The brainstorm hit me without warning. That camera was a real break! If I remembered right, the kit held another roll of infra-red film.

And since I'd only used eight bulbs out of a box of a dozen, there would be four bulbs left.

I could go back to the plant and get those pictures tonight. It couldn't be more than ten-thirty. Devlin's gang would still be working.

I slipped out of bed and began dressing. It wasn't easy in the dark and I made some noise, I guess, but Brains never even stirred.

Once I was dressed, I took the bag with the camera and slipped toward the wide-open window.

Brains only used this window as an emergency exit. But this was an emergency!

There was a box beneath the window. I opened it and took out the rolled-up rope ladder that Brains always kept ready. Somehow I managed to attach one end to a couple of hooks that Brains had screwed beneath the sill. Then I lowered the ladder gently through the window.

With the kit slung on my shoulder, I went over the sill. Climbing downward, I thought of leaving Brains a note, but that would only mean delay. Besides, if everything went well, I ought to be back before midnight with some real evidence. I could tell Brains then.

Minutes later I was wheeling out of Crestwood and heading for Bleeker City.

I wasn't sure if I could find the route by myself, but I did. I guess some of that "seeing-eye stuff" was rubbing off on me. But believe me, I sure missed Brains just the same.

Most folks in Bleeker City had gone to sleep and almost all the lights were out. It was mighty spooky riding up those dark, silent back streets, I can tell you.

But it got even spookier out in the open country. I had my headlight on part of the way. But as I got closer to the plant, I had to switch it off.

After that, there was only the faint reflection of the white center strip in the road to guide me.

But finally I topped the last rise. Below me in the darkness was a huge pool of deeper shadow.

I was there! The plant was just ahead, waiting for me.

And for all I knew so were Devlin and his gang!

It took every ounce of will power to walk down those last few hundred feet to the entrance of the driveway, but I did it! I *had* to! I wasn't going to fumble the ball again.

Ducking behind the sign, I eased my bike down in the high grass. I had loaded my camera by the light of a street lamp in Bleeker City. Now, there was nothing left to do but soft-shoe down the driveway and get those pictures!

I'd been this way before. It hadn't been easy with Brains beside me. It was a lot harder now that I was alone. But even though my legs were shaking like jelly, I somehow made it.

As I came up along the side of the building, I could hear the press thumping. That meant Devlin and his bunch were still working. I'd be sure to get the pictures.

Exactly how it happened I couldn't tell you. I had my camera aimed at the window and ready for the first shot when suddenly I heard a crunch of gravel behind me.

I started to whip around! Someone grabbed me from behind!

A big hammy hand clapped across my mouth and cut off my yell.

My legs churned madly but that didn't help either. I wasn't going anywhere.

*I was a dead pigeon and I knew it!*

# 24 CAPTURED!

My heart was beating like a jungle tom-tom. I kept trying to break free, but I was being carried under someone's arm like a bundle of washing.

The guy lugging me started to yell. "Bunko! Whisper! Quick! Get out here!"

That booming voice was the giveaway! It was Devlin who had grabbed me. He was holding me tighter than a strait jacket and I could smell the odor of old cigar tobacco on the hand across my mouth.

A second later Devlin had dragged me inside the house. He let me down but held on to me by the back of my collar.

Whisper and four or five other rough-looking, bullet-headed guys crowded around. They all looked like bad actors.

"And you guys said I was hearing things," sneered Devlin. "I told you I heard someone out there snooping around before."

He glared at me. "I figured one of them might be dumb enough to come back, and I was laying for him."

*Dumb enough!* Brother, that was me all right!

Whisper yanked the camera and the kit out of my hands. "A flash gun and infra-red bulbs! The little snoop has been taking pictures, Boss."

He opened the back of the camera and ripped out the film.

That's when Devlin slammed me up against a wall near the press.

"I warned you to stay away, squirt, but you just had to come back, didn't you? Well, you'll be good and sorry."

Devlin wasn't pulling his big-brother act now.

He sounded like a big bull gorilla, roaring mad. From behind him there were four other big apes who looked like they were just itching to get at me.

I should have been scared silly. And I was. But I was mad too. I started to yell right back at Devlin.

"All right, so you caught me. But it won't do you any good. We've got enough evidence to put you and your gang in jail."

Devlin shoved his head forward. "We—eh? Guess you mean that redheaded string bean you hang around with, the Benton kid."

He grabbed me by the front of my jacket and pulled me forward, right up against his face.

"All right, tell me where he is, or I'll fix your wagon here and now."

"He's busy developing another roll of infra-red film," I lied brazenly. "We've got a photo record of this whole plant. We know all about that Curio Shop, too. And we even have a copy of that big coin you're planning to counterfeit, the decadrachm! And when Brains turns that all over to the police—"

He shoved me away. "When he turns it over? That means he hasn't done it yet!"

Devlin turned to his gang. "Looks as if we're in a jam here, boys. I don't know how these kids got all that dope on us, but if they haven't given it to the cops yet, we still have time!"

"Time for what?" Whisper asked, his voice low and husky. "We can't hang around here waiting for the cops to nab us."

"Look," Devlin snapped, "I've got a fortune tied up here in supplies, equipment, and finished coins. We could get it cleaned up and on the truck in a couple of hours."

"He's right," said Whisper. "Then, even if they do come here, the cops won't have a shred of evidence left."

"Okay, let's go!" Devlin said. He began to bawl orders. "Bunko, take a man and start taking apart the press! Hickey, you and Brun start cooling off the smelter, so we can dismantle it. Whisper, grab a car and warn Gorme! Tell him to pack up his tools and dies and get them over here before dawn!"

With all that hullabaloo, I thought they'd forgotten all about me. I started easing for the door, planning to make a break for it, but Whisper grabbed me.

"What about this little brat?" he said. "He ought to get paid off."

"Not now," said Devlin. "Tie him up and heave him into a closet. We'll attend to him later."

Whisper had me tied hand and foot in a second. Then he dragged me into the next room, opened up a door and shoved me into the darkness.

I remember tripping and falling. Then my head hit something —and I didn't remember anything for a long time.

I came to with a terrific headache. My noggin felt as if someone was running an egg beater inside.

But after a while everything stopped spinning. I found myself leaning against a wall. There was a window way over my head, and by the faint light coming in through the window I could see the wall opposite me was no more than four feet away, so I knew I was in some kind of closet.

I could hear the gang outside the closet door. Devlin was barking orders and there was the sound of hammers and wrenches. I heard Gorme's voice too, so I knew that he'd cleared out of the Curio Shop and come here to join the others.

Well, maybe I was just a snooping kid but I sure had lit a fire under Devlin and his gang.

Then it hit me! Sure I'd scared them. Scared them into a get-away, just when we had the goods on them! Now, thanks to me, they would be out of the state by the time the police came and found me.

*If* they came and *if* they found me!

The thought of that big *if* chilled me. I hadn't told anyone where I was going. It might take weeks before someone thought of looking for me here. By that time it would be . . . too late!

That was if Devlin left me here alive in the first place. But I didn't want to think about that.

I heard somebody yelling. "Okay, Devlin, we've got the press on the truck. The stuff in the shack is being loaded right now. What's next?"

"Get the dies and the finished coins and load them in my car. Work fast! It's almost dawn! We want to be out of here when they come looking for that kid."

I glanced at the window. It looked a lot lighter up there. Daylight would be here soon.

"What *about* that kid?" asked Whisper, thinly.

"Don't worry," said Devlin. "I'll fix him before we go!"

Then, all at once, I heard another voice. But it didn't come from inside the house like the others. It had a sort of booming echo to it, and it sounded as if it came from outside and behind the house.

"Attention, Devlin! Attention! You are under close observation. You cannot hope to get away with this. Your doom is sealed."

That voice! Sure it was loud and booming. But with that kind of language, I'd eat my hat if it didn't sound like Brains Benton!

The booming voice cut out sharply. What had happened? Where did he go? If it was Brains, where did he get a voice as loud as that? My head was beginning to spin again. Then, without warning, I heard another booming announcement.

"Attention, Devlin! We have all the evidence we need to convict you and your gang. You cannot escape your fate!"

Outside the door in the plant there was silence now. And then, all of a sudden, Devlin was snapping questions. "What's going on out there, Whisper?"

"It's someone out in the woods behind the shack," came the answer. "I think he's trying to scare us into making a run for it."

"Well, what are we waiting for?" said Devlin. "Let's go out there and grab him!"

I heard the sound of running feet as they left the house.

Then the mysterious voice was booming again.

"Devlin, release your prisoner at once. Harm a hair of his head and you are doomed. Any attempt at escape is futile!"

I could hear the shouting voices of Devlin and his men as they scoured the woods.

"Brains," I groaned. The big jerk had risked his life to come and rescue me. If they ever found him it would be his finish too.

Suddenly I detected a faint scraping sound. Like somebody moving cautiously.

Then out of the clear blue came a hoarse whisper. "Jimmy! Jimmy, where are you?"

It was *Brains!*

"Brains," I yelled. "I'm here! In the closet."

In an instant the closet door swung open and there was Brains kneeling beside me slashing at my ropes with a penknife.

At that very moment I heard the booming voice again, echoing from the woods. "Devlin! You have done your last evil deed. Prepare to face justice! You must pay the penalty in full!"

"Brains!" I gasped, as he cut me free. "How can you be out there and in here at the same time?"

"I'll explain later," he snapped. "Right now, we've got to get out of here, and *fast!*"

He helped me to my feet. I had a little trouble walking, but we started for the back door. Outside the voice was sounding off again. "Devlin, you cannot escape. You must pay your debt to society . . . !"

All of a sudden the voice was cut off with a strangled squawk.

I didn't get it at all. I hobbled after Brains, my head spinning like crazy.

We had just made it to the door. It looked as if we'd make a clean getaway when suddenly Gorme, Whisper and four others of the gang came pouring out of the woods and into the yard.

We were cut off! Gorme was smiling wolfishly and in his hand he held—of all things—a tape recorder!

"I might have known it would be that young redheaded smart-aleck," he said, glaring at Brains. "He used that tape recorder to trick us out into the woods while he sneaked in here and turned his pal loose."

Gorme dropped the tape recorder on the ground. "Well, it didn't quite work!" he said. "And now we've got both of you!"

"Mr. Gorme," said Brains disapprovingly, "you really shouldn't be so careless with my equipment."

Grimly Gorme advanced toward us. "Wise guy, eh? Okay, boys," he said. "Let's fix these meddling kids right now!"

## 25 ENTER THE POLICE

"Touch those kids and I'll ram your teeth down your throat, Gorme!" came a voice echoing from the corner of the yard.

I whipped around. There, at the end of the driveway, stood two policemen with revolvers in their hands. One of them was our old friend, Officer Burney.

It was just like the old-time movies when the U.S. Cavalry arrived in the nick of time. I knew things didn't happen that way. I was positive that it was all a dream and I'd wake up screaming. But no kidding, it was for real.

"Cops!" squawked Gorme. He ducked and headed for the other side of the house.

"Don't bother," called Burney. "We've got that side covered too!"

Sure enough, Gorme came back dragged by two big men in blue. One of them was a sergeant. Gorme didn't look tough at all now. Just scared.

"Which one of you is the Benton boy?" asked the sergeant.

"I am, sir," answered Brains. "If you'll look in that truck I believe you'll find all the evidence I spoke to you about over the phone a while ago. . . . However, the chief culprit is still missing. I believe Mr. Devlin may be hiding out there in the woods."

That's about when two more policemen came out of the woods hauling Devlin between them.

"We found this one heading for the swamp, Sarge," reported one of the officers.

Devlin sputtered indignantly. "Sergeant, this is a colossal mistake. I don't know what these crazy kids have told you, but I had nothing to do with whatever was going on here."

Brains snatched a handful of photographs from his pocket.

"Mr. Devlin," said Brains, "I have here the most conclusive evidence of your criminal activities! These eight flash photographs prove beyond a doubt you are the brains behind this whole operation."

It was as if we'd knocked the wind out of him. Devlin stopped blustering. I guess he'd never run into anything like Brains Benton before—and it was just too much for him.

"All right," he mumbled. "You win! I'll sign a confession."

"Might as well," said a voice behind him. It was Gorme. "I wasn't going to go to the pen without you to keep me company."

"Let's go, men!" said the sergeant. "We don't want to keep Judge Parker waiting."

As they loaded the gang into a couple of squad cars, the sergeant told us we wouldn't be needed at court till tomorrow. But we could expect a visit from the District Attorney for a statement.

As the police started away, they offered us a lift but Brains said no, we'd ride our bikes in together.

Actually we didn't need those bikes at all. We floated home on a cloud.

On the way back to Bleeker City, Brains filled me in.

The rope ladder slamming against the wall of the house had awakened Brains before dawn. The ladder told him that I was gone. The missing camera told him where, and his watch told him for how long.

"I figured they'd probably captured you and were keeping you at the plant," said Brains. "That's why I brought that battery-powered tape recorder along. I used that spiel to lure them away from the house and give me a chance to come looking for you."

"But good golly," I said. "Were we ever lucky that the police came when they did!"

Brains glanced over at me and he was smiling a little. "Lucky?" he said. "It was more than blind luck, Operative Three. You see, I was partway through Bleeker City when I realized I was making the same mistake you had made—going on a dangerous mission without telling anyone about it. That's when I found an all-night diner and called the police. Fortunately, Officer Burney was on desk duty and he responded nobly."

"I'll say he did," I put in.

"Meanwhile I went ahead to the plant," Brains continued, "and tied my tape recorder high up in a tree in the woods behind the house. I turned it on full power and a timing device did the rest."

I shook my head trying to take it all in. "But Brains," I said, "where did you get the nerve to flash those so-called photographs? You knew the shots we took were blanks!"

"Yes, but Devlin didn't—and his confession is all we need for a conviction."

Well, what could I say after that? Where do you find the words to thank a guy for getting you out of that kind of a jam? All I could do was mumble, "Thanks, Brains."

He didn't answer, just gave me a big grin.

On the way through Bleeker City we stopped to tell Terry and her father the good news. But Officer Burney had already been to the Dexter house and given them most of the details.

Terry and Mr. Dexter could hardly find the words to thank us. But then Terry got kind of mad.

"Jimmy! Why did you go back there by yourself? You should have had someone else along! You know I would have been glad to help."

Good gravy! What would I want her along for! I did a pretty good job of bungling all by myself!

After that Brains and I headed home for Crestwood, riding on top of the world. But when we arrived at the Benton house the roof fell in.

Mrs. Benton was half hysterical. She had found Brains' bedroom empty and was sure that we'd either run away from home or had been kidnapped. We both tried to explain all the details of what had happened to Mrs. Benton and Brains' father, too. But we weren't making much headway until Mr. Frazer, the District Attorney, arrived in a car with the County Seal on the door, followed by three reporters and two photographers.

After that, everything was easier. Especially when the D.A. brought out the information that Devlin had made a full confession, and so had Gorme and the rest of the gang. Not that the police needed it, because they had all the captured equipment and the counterfeits as evidence.

Besides that, the police had found Devlin's list of contacts, the crooked dealers who sold his fake coins. They had notified the authorities of a dozen countries, some as far away as Switzerland. They expected to round up the entire ring in short order.

Well, after we had made our statements to Mr. Frazer, he let the reporters in. We were photographed and questioned. But I made sure my favorite paper, the *Crestwood Daily Ledger*, got an exclusive interview.

Right after that, I got a call telling me to go straight home. My family had arrived.

Naturally I scooted home to tell them the story. Dad, Mother and Ann had already heard some of it on the car radio. That's why they'd hurried back to Crestwood, not even stopping for lunch. But just the same everyone wanted to hear the details, so I was in my glory.

I was too wound up to take my newspaper route that day so I called Mr. Worts, the circulation manager, and he said he'd get Stinky Green to handle it for me.

The excitement started all over again when the *Ledger* came out. There was this banner headline across the top:

## YOUNG SHERLOCKS TRAP COUNTERFEITERS
### CRESTWOOD SLEUTHS SMASH INTERNATIONAL RING!

And right beneath it were the pictures they'd taken of Brains and me. Yipes! You should have seen that shot. I had the silliest grin on my face.

And there was a picture of Jeremy Dexter and his daughter Terry. My father said the publicity would give the Dexter store a big boost. After what Jeremy Dexter and Terry had been through, he sure deserved a break like that.

Finally my mother ordered the papers cleared away and she set the table. She said there had been enough excitement for one day and she wanted everyone to settle down to supper.

By then I was bushed and the thought of a relaxed evening sounded like heaven.

But do you know what happened?

We were just finishing dessert when the doorbell rang. Ann went to answer it. She came back with a bewildered look on her face and an envelope in her hand. A *red envelope*.

"There wasn't anyone there," she said. "Just this envelope under the door. It's not addressed!"

"Let me see it," said my father.

He took the envelope and opened it. And, as he read the small piece of paper inside, a dazed look crossed his face too.

"Nothing in here but a few words," he said, puzzled. "It says 'Satellite Zeta is in orbit.' Must be some kind of a nut that wrote it."

I nearly choked on the piece of pie I was eating.

The code signal! I'd have to go to headquarters at once!

Getting out of the house wasn't too easy, but at last my father said, "Well, all right, but don't stay long. You've had a big day, son."

I streaked for the lab with a hundred questions whirling in my brain. Why hadn't Brains called me on the phone in the usual way? And if he'd come to my house, why hadn't he asked to speak to me instead of leaving that note? And if it had been somebody else who'd delivered it—then *who?* And *why?* And what was the idea of that *red envelope?*

You could see there were a lot of mysterious angles. And to top it all—with only two days left of our Easter vacation—any new case would have to be solved on a crash basis.

But we could do it if we tried.

In an emergency like this Benton and Carson could depend on all its investigators—especially Operative Three.

# Whitman CLASSICS

The Hound of the
  Baskervilles

Tales to Tremble By

More Tales to Tremble By

Seven Great Detective
  Stories

Black Beauty

Tales From Arabian Nights

Little Women

The Call of the Wild

Tom Sawyer

Robin Hood

The Wonderful Wizard
  of Oz

Robinson Crusoe

Wild Animals I Have
  Known

The War of the Worlds

Stand By for Adventure

Huckleberry Finn

Alice in Wonderland

*Start your home library of*
*WHITMAN CLASSICS now.*

# Whitman ADVENTURE and MYSTERY Books

## SPORTS STORIES
Throw the Long Bomb
Hot Rod Road

## BRAINS BENTON
The Missing Message
The Counterfeit Coin
The Stolen Dummy
The Roving Rolls
The Waltzing Mouse
The Painted Dragon

## DONNA PARKER
At Cherrydale
Special Agent
On Her Own

## WALT DISNEY PRESENTS
Peter Pan
The Gnome-Mobile
The Swiss Family
Robinson

## TELEVISION FAVORITES
The Mod Squad

Land of the Giants

Ironside

Mission: Impossible

Star Trek

Hawaii Five-O

The High Chaparral

The Rat Patrol

Garrison's Gorillas

The Monkees

Bonanza

Lassie
*Bristlecone Pine*
*Smelters' Cave*

The Invaders

Gunsmoke

Whitman

REG. U.S. PAT. OFF.